The
Problim
Children

The
Problim
Children

NATALIE LLOYD

KT KATHERINE TEGEN BOOKS
An Imprint of HarperCollins Publishers

Katherine Tegen Books is an imprint of HarperCollins Publishers.

The Problim Children
Text and illustrations copyright © 2018 by HarperCollins Publishers
All rights reserved. Printed in the United States of America.
No part of this book may be used or reproduced in any manner whatsoever
without written permission except in the case of brief quotations embodied in
critical articles and reviews. For information address HarperCollins Children's
Books, a division of HarperCollins Publishers, 195 Broadway, New York, NY
10007.
www.harpercollinschildrens.com

ISBN 978-0-06-242820-2

Typography by Carla Weise
17 18 19 20 21   PC/LSCH   10 9 8 7 6 5 4 3 2 1
❖
First Edition

FOR ANDY ASBURY,
not because he's a problem child
(even though the Problims would love him).
But because he's brave and funny and awesome.
(And because I love him too.)

Mona Problim

Monday's child
is fair of face,

Tuesday's child
is full of grace,

Toot Problim

Wendell Problim

Wednesday's child
is full of woe,

Thursday's child
has far to go,

Thea Problim

Friday's child is
loving and giving,

Frida Problim

Sal Problim

Saturday's child works
hard for a living,

Sundae Problim

But the child who's born
on the Sabbath day is
good and wise in every way.

—Anonymous

Prologue

O nce upon a Wednesday, many years ago, a small boy made a brave decision.

Somewhere in the deep woods of the Carolinas, he ran, breathless. The brave boy's heart never steadied until he reached the top of the cold rock hill. His sister waited for him there, and he flung his arms around her waist and hugged her tight. She motioned the rest of their siblings out from the cave where they'd been hiding.

She pushed the boy an arm's length away and stared deep into his eyes. "You sure about this?" she asked.

The little boy nodded. "We hide it. And we don't tell anybody about it, no matter what."

They walked out to the cliff's edge together, to stare down over the wild river below. Fog billowed like dragon's breath across the wrinkled water.

Soon, a boat full of shadowed figures sailed through the mist. A long-haired man stood tall at the front of the boat, his jacket rippling in the wind. *Cheese Breath*, the boy had called him. He thought it was only the man's breath that reeked when he promised the children glory and riches. But now he knew that man's heart was rotten too. Cheese Breath was determined to find a treasure rumored to be better than silver or gold. He would destroy anything, or anyone, who stood in front of it.

The boy tucked his hand inside his big sister's. Then the rest of his siblings took their places, locking muddy fingers until they stood together, side by side, in a firm line called family that could not be moved or shaken.

"Ready?" the oldest girl asked.

The children nodded, shivering in the cold.

The girl closed her eyes, and the sky woke up.

Silver swirled with black storm clouds. The ground shook and cracked. The mighty river curled its tongue, burying the boat in its depths.

Another boy watched from the woods that day, eyes wide. Heart racing. "Until the seven do return," he mumbled the words of the old rhyme. He couldn't believe what he'd just seen.

Maybe some legends are strange enough to be true.

Kaboom Day

Nobody in the town of Lost Cove ever stomped their muddy boots near the Swampy Woods. They knew those woods were dark and haunted (probably) and always covered in a strange fog. That fog has teeth, the locals said. That fog'll snap at you! So everybody stayed out. And this was perfectly agreeable to the only family brave enough to live in such a wretched place. For many years, this abysmal swamp (full of mud-spiders, fanged fog, and wattabats) had been the private paradise of the Problim family.

But all good things—even if they are good in a terrible way—have a habit of coming to an end.

On the seventh day of the seventh month, Sal Problim stepped out of his family's crumbly bungalow and took in his surroundings. Fog billowed around the rickety front porch. Bullfrogs hollered *yerrrp* from somewhere deep in the woods. Heavy-bellied rain clouds floating overhead kept the sunlight from sneaking through. Sal smiled and said, "Beautiful."

And then a smell somewhat between rotten eggs and vomit singed his nose hairs.

Sal pulled the collar of his shirt over his nose. "Toot? Where are you?"

Ichabod, the family's pet pig, waddled out the front door of the bungalow squealing *ork-ork-ork*! Riding astride the swine was a toddler wearing a striped onesie and Velcro bow tie. Wafting around this smallest Problim was his own unique fog . . . of stink. Toot Problim's farts were so varied and precise that the Problim children had assigned each one a number for categorization purposes.

As the pig bounded toward Sal, Toot bounced on its back, puffing a series of warning farts. All #4s.[1]

---

1 #4: The Stink of Dread: A fart born of anxiety, foretelling a terrible event. Smells faintly of rotten eggs and vomit.

Sal's nose wrinkled. "You should get an award for that one. It's stanktastic. What's got you worried?"

But then Sal remembered what day it was. Sunday. *Her* day. The day his oldest sister forced all her siblings to take a bath. "Tooty-kins," called a sunshiny voice from inside. "Your turn!"

"It's okay, kid," Sal said with a shiver. "I'll launch you into the woods!" Sal swooped up his baby brother and bounded down the steps, headed for the human catapult his siblings kept in the yard. As Sal ran, the tools hanging from his sleeves made a rustling, metallic sound. A small rake, a shovel, razor-sharp shears, and trowels all clinked, scraped, and tinged as he moved.

But Toot shook his head and pointed to the ground.

"Oh!" Sal jumped as a cool, slimy tangle of ivy brushed past his ankle. More ivy, green tendrils—long and thin as spaghetti noodles—crept through the fog and toward the front porch. The plant was moving fast. He'd never seen it do this before, and that frustrated him. At thirteen, Sal—Saturday's child—thrived on hard work and was an astute gardener. He specialized in strange, exotic, and smelly plants. But this was an anomaly.

"Weird," Sal said as long vines of Wrangling Ivy slithered up the porch steps. If Sal had engineered the planting just right—and he always did—the Wrangling Ivy would eventually grow a hundred feet long. It would be able to trap a human and pull him or her zigzaggedly across the garden. He sighed with longing as he imagined the ivy catching his siblings someday.

Catching. Not creeping—which is what the ivy was doing now.

Up the porch.

Up the house.

Slithering through the upstairs window.

"What are you *doing*?" Sal shouted.

The plant didn't answer, of course.

But Sundae Problim did. She burst through the halfway-open door wearing a yellow smiley-face T-shirt, faded denim shorts, and her usual sparkly smile. "Problims, pile up!" she shouted. "Let's play a game called 'CLEAN THE HOUSE SPOTLESS'!"

And, with that, the house blew up.

BOOOOOOM!

The noise was so loud and sharp that it sounded as if someone had whacked the sky with an ax.

Suddenly and quite efficiently, the entire bunga-low began to fold inward like a deck of cards . . . a deck of cards with lots of glass and nails holding it together. Ivy snapped around Sal's ankle and yanked him to the ground just as a shard of glass sailed past his face. More ivy snapped down around each Problim—boy, toddler, pig, Sundae—and yanked them in a quick streak across the garden, toward the shelter of the trees.

Toot squealed happily.

Sundae screamed with joy.

Ichabod *ork*ed!

Sal watched debris flying overhead—furniture legs, a pie pan, the lava lamp he'd just gotten from the dump—dang it—plus one wild-haired sister: Thea Problim. Her black curls billowed as she clawed the air. Their home, plus Sal's beautiful garden, was now a rubble pile.

Toot clapped solemnly as if he'd just watched an interesting play. He straightened his bow tie and puffed a #17.[2] He followed with another #4.

<hr>

2 **#17**: The Pompous Fart: Means: I told you so. Smells like a clogged garbage disposal, plus the faintest trace of lemon.

Thursday's Child

The world looks weirdly awesome upside down, Thea Problim decided. For seven seconds, she allowed herself to imagine a flip-flopped world—where people rode bicycles, square-danced, and wrestled alligators in the sky. *Gosh, that'd be beautiful!* But this—this *mess* all around her—was not beautiful. Sure, on most days, rubble piles were fabulous. But today, Thea knew it was the beginning of something rotten.

Everything is changing. Those words kept falling over Thea's heart like a picnic blanket on a muddy field.

"I saw three sevens in the stars!" she shouted to

her siblings. "And this morning, I saw three more of them!"

Sal groaned. "Not this again."

"Is this a new game?" Sundae squealed, ignoring her sister. Despite the fact that they'd all just been in an explosion, Sundae's voice sounded like wind chimes on a warm summer day. "Sal! Tooty-kins! Did you two *kaboom* the house? Tell me how to play!"

Sal wiped the dust out of his eyes. "Why would I kaboom the house and destroy my garden? *And* our human catapult?"

Sundae clapped her hands together, sending tiny puffs of dust around her face. "What a fun adventure!" She skipped back toward the rubble. "Problims! Pile up!"

"Fine. Don't listen to me," Thea sighed, dangling from above, watching her siblings run off. "Nobody ever does. Wait, Sal! Talk to your plant! Make it put me down! I need to find Wendell and tell him we're doomed."

Before Sal could respond, the ivy around Thea unspooled, sending her spiraling face-first into the mud. He scrambled to help her up. At nearly twelve, Thea was only two years younger than Sal but several inches taller. She looked over Sal's shoulder and realized—for the first time—that their entire home really was a scrap pile of wood.

Three sevens, she thought.

What if something terrible happened to Wendell?

Thea ran for the rubble pile, hurdling chunks of roof, pots and pans, and pieces of furniture. Toot rode the pig beside her, a stick extended before him like a joust.

"Wendell!" Thea called. "Where are you?" Panic squeezed her heart.

Thump, *bump*. Thea sighed with relief.

Wendell was alive, at least, wherever he was. For as long as she could remember, Thea had heard the echo of her twin's heartbeat after her own. Heartspeak, they called it. He'd been her best friend since the days they were born—seven pounds each, seven minutes apart. Wendell on a Wednesday. Thea on a Thursday.

Thea scampered squirrel-fast across the rubble, toward the corner of the house where she thought their bedroom used to be. She pressed her hand against her pounding chest.

I'm coming, she heartspoke. *Twins for the win!*

Thump, *bump*.

It's okay, she felt him say. *I'm cool.*

A scrawny arm shot up from the debris waving an old, gray T-shirt like a flag, along with the muffled voice of Wendell. "Am I d-dreaming?"

Thea felt seven trillion times stronger than usual as she hurled a patch of roof out of the way, Sal and Sundae close behind to help. Strands of Wrangling Ivy had twined together in a canopy covering Wendell. He pushed through the vines, grabbed Thea's arm, and climbed out.

"I was so afraid," Thea said, throwing her arms around him.

"You're always af-fraid," Wendell said, his voice muffled against her shirt.

Thea pushed her brother at arm's length so she could assess his appearance. Wendell's glasses were twisted sideways on his face, which was typically how he wore them anyway. He had the same dark hair and dark eyes as his twin. But he also had a distinct reddish-purple birthmark on the right side of his face. The mark spread from underneath his eye to the middle of his cheek. He held a book in his arms like a teddy bear, cuddled tightly against his chest. He looked around . . . puzzled. And he simply said, "W-wow. Looks like we're homeless now. What's for breakfast?"

Before Thea could answer, Sal rushed past her, running for the leaning tower of chimney. "Hold on, Frida!"

A small, scrawny girl in jeans, suspenders, and a striped hoodie—complete with fox ears—gripped the brick pile. She wore an orange backpack strapped to her shoulders and a radiant smile on her face. She cheered as her siblings raced toward her. She shouted proudly:

> "*The fox survives!*
> *The fox prevails!*
> *Has anybody seen my tail?*"

Thea reached for her little sister and pulled her into her arms for a hug.

"We might have to make you a new tail," Thea said, kissing the top of Frida's head. "Now let's find Mona."

"Oh, isn't this sooo much fun?" Sundae cooed as she skipped up behind them. "It's like a wonderful game of hide-and-seek!"

"You found me then." The wind carried Mona's voice from the woods. Just the sound of it made the hair on Thea's neck go prickly stiff. Mona's voice was as lovely as the rest of her; made for storytelling and song-sharing. But Mona's family knew her voice was full of secrets. And plots. And evil, really.

"That explosion was marvelous," Mona said as she flicked open a black umbrella to shield her pet Venus flytrap from fluttering scraps of debris. The pink flowerpot was nestled over Mona's heart, in a baby sling that the family had originally bought for Toot. Even Sal, who loved plants, was creeped out by the flytrap's frozen grin.

Mona smirked and looked at Sal. "Good job."

"Why does everybody think it's *me*?" Sal shouted. "Why would I kaboom the house and ruin my own garden?"

"Because you ruin everything," Mona said.

Thea jumped between her siblings. "Please, guys! It scares me when you two—"

"*You* blew up my garden." Sal glared at Mona.

Mona smiled sweetly. She fluttered her eyelashes. "Everything happens for a reason."

"That's the spirit, Mona!" Sundae cooed.

Sal pushed past Thea so he could yell in Mona's face. And then Mona was shouting at him and Toot was riding the pig in circles (farting squirty-sounding

#40s[3]) and Frida was climbing one of the tall trees, mumbling:

"Adventure on a whim;

Fox on a limb!"

Sundae was spinning in circles, singing a ridiculous song about joy and love while the ruins smoked behind her. Wendell sat, legs crossed, on the ground, reading his muddy book.

"Wendell," Thea whispered, flopping down beside him. "Everybody's acting so *normal*. But we have a serious predicament."

Thump, *bump*. He shrugged. "It was just the house."

"It's not just the house . . . ," Thea said.

But maybe that was part of it, she thought as she looked over the debris. Now their home was a heap of boards. A billow of smoke. How was that possible, Thea wondered. That one minute you could have a home, and the next minute your home was simply a swamp-heap of kaboom dust? She liked rubble, of course. The Problim children had kaboomed plenty

---

3 **#40**: The Jouster: A trumpetous rally Toot toots when riding Ichabod. Smells faintly of smoke and rotten fruit.

of things in the past. But this time was different. This was their home. And now it was . . .

Smooshed.

Squished.

Gone.

Everything was changing.

And this was only the beginning.

"We're just h-homeless." Wendell shrugged.

Homeless, Thea realized. What a lonely sounding word. And what if they couldn't get in touch with their parents now? For the Problim family, few things were really emergency worthy. Sundae took care of them while their parents were gone on work adventures, and they all took care of one another and were unschooled together. But now the Help Phone was buried somewhere beneath the rubble.

And where would they sleep? Camping was fun for a while, but the wattabats liked to bite this time of year.

"It's not the house," she said, leaning closer to him. "I'm afraid something has happened . . . to Mom and Dad. I'm seeing sevens, Wendell. That's what I've been trying to tell everyone. We haven't heard from Mom and Dad in seven weeks—not by mail or email or phone or anything—and sevens are popping up everywhere!"

Thump, *bump*. Wendell closed the book in his lap and gave his sister his full attention now.

Because when you are a Problim and sevens start piling up, trouble's headed in your direction.

A Sudden Splash
of Purple

"And another seven appeared last night. You fell asleep with your shoes on and kicked them off the top bunk. I was sleeping on the floor. And one hit my head here, see?" Thea pointed to a tiny purple bruise above her eyebrow. "It's a seven shape!"

"I'm s-sorry." Wendell realized he was only wearing one red sneaker. "You're sleeping on the floor again? Really, Thea? The bottom bunk isn't low enough to the ground?"

"I prefer sleeping on the floor. Midge Lodestar says the best way to overcome a fear of heights is by keeping your head on the ground."

Frida the Fox turned a cartwheel, plopping down

beside them in the mud. "Who is Midge Lodestar?"

"My life coach," Thea said happily.

Wendell shook his head. "She's a DJ on the country classics channel on Dad's old radio. Thea listens every night."

"*You* should listen," Thea told him. "Midge even has a mantra for when she's afraid. She says, when you're fearful, you take a deep breath, release it slowly and say: Every day is a good day for a taco."

Frida nodded. "Brilliant."

Wendell shook his head. "That doesn't make sense."

"It does to me! I think of tacos and I'm less afraid. A little bit. Maybe."

Thea Problim had loads of phobias. But the kind of fear that overwhelmed her when her parents were gone on a mission—that was the worst. She was afraid to say it out loud, even. Because what if saying a terrible thing gave it power somehow—sealed it like a bad wish bound to come true?

"They're always c-careful," Wendell said softly.

"Careful and safe aren't the same thing."

"Problims!" Sundae chirped, clapping her hands. "Let's focus. Explosions are nature's way of telling us to start over. So let's make the best of this!

We should rebuild the house, right? We can probably have it finished before Mom and Dad get home. How hard can it be?"

At exactly that moment, the post that had been holding up the front porch crashed to the ground.

Sundae beamed. "We get to start completely from scratch!"

Sal was already scaling the rubble, taking measurements in his mind. "It's blown to bits." He pulled a tape measure from his tool belt and slid it across the broken boards. "It could take years to reframe it."

"Too bad you didn't think of that before you destroyed it," Mona mumbled.

"I didn't do this," Sal shouted. "YOU did!"

Mona flicked her hair behind her shoulder, and added softly, "Things happen. There is always a cause. And an effect."

"No matter!" Sundae added, with a whistle to get everyone's attention. "It's done! What's the family motto?"

Toot clapped and trumpeted a splattery-sounding #211.[4]

---

4 **#211**: The Motto Fart: A flatulent trumpet of declaration embracing Toot's life philosophy: fart loudly and proudly and be brave and courageous.

Frida leaped to attention, raised her hand in the air and said:

"The baby flatulates!
The fox translates:
Fart loudly and proudly and be brave and
*   courageous!"*

"That is *Toot's* motto." Sundae patted his shoulder. "The family motto is: every Problim is a gift!"

"Sundae," Sal said as he tried to salvage his plants from underneath the rubble, "you're giving me a happiness headache."

Before Thea could chime in, a strange sight caught her eye—a swoosh of purple scurrying low to the ground.

Flickering through the fog.

Skirting along the rubble.

Bouncing on a window frame.

Thea squeezed her eyes shut tight. Maybe seeing an implosion had the same effect on her mind as staring at the sun too long—maybe she was seeing blur-spots of light. But when she blinked her eyes open wide . . . she saw purple. Again!

Thea elbowed Wendell and pointed.

Thump, *bump*. He'd seen it too.

Weirder still, Thea heard a melody—a faint and twinkling kind of tune, like the faraway sound of a music box.

There is nothing in the world—no box, no safe, no diary—that keeps a memory as well hidden as a song. So Thea's heart ballooned full of all kinds of feelings: excitement and sadness and wonder. That song had unlocked the edge of a memory that she could almost grasp. Almost . . .

Tell me a tale worth telling back. The lyric drifted across her mind. Thea gasped softly and looked at Wendell.

His eyes were wide and extra big behind his glasses. Those eyes were glossed over with a far-away, dreamy look, the kind of look you get when you think about birthdays and snow days and people you love. He was remembering too.

Thea leaned in and whispered, "You hear the music?"

Wendell nodded.

"Where's it from?" she whispered, stepping closer to the rubble, following that strange, familiar song.

"Careful," Wendell called out. "You're not w-wearing shoes."

Thea paused; she didn't need to go farther anyway. She saw it clearly: the purple swoosh was actually a fluffy purple tail belonging to a squirrel. A silver squirrel. A squirrel that looked more like a tiny robot than an animal.

The Swampy Woods were full of wondrous creatures. But she'd never seen anything like this.

Her heart soared. "Hi," she said softly.

The squirrel regarded her quite calmly, tilting its head. Studying her. Thea saw a strange sparkle in one of the squirrel's eyes, a special gleam, like the kind of light that shimmers from twinkling stars, or from shiny ribbons on a Christmas present.

"I've got it!" Sundae shouted.

And with a flick of its tail, the squirrel—or whatever it was—ran away.

Sundae squealed and clapped her hands. "I know the answer to our problems, Problims! Find shovels, rakes, anything that can help us dig!" Sundae hoisted Toot up on her hip.

Mona beamed. "Are we burying someone? I vote Sal."

"No," Sundae said. "But I do know the answer to this problem. And it's buried on Oak Tree Hill."

Sir Frank's Metal
Lunch Box

Each time Wendell Problim's shovel hit the ground he thought about pancakes.

Blueberry pancakes. *Thunk.*

Apple-cranberry-compote pancakes. *Thunk.*

The Problim family loved eating pancakes, and Wendell loved making them. That had been his plan that morning. He'd had the most wonderful dream about water. Again. This time he was surfing. Balanced on a wild, foamy wave, he crept higher and higher and . . .

Then he woke up. He thought about equally exciting endeavors—breakfast!—and then the ceiling had collapsed in his face.

"This is like d-digging through chocolate ice cream to get to a dark-chocolate c-cookie," he said. "I h-hope the end result is just as w-wonderful." Wendell wiped sweat from his forehead. "What exactly are we looking for, Sundae? S-Sundae?"

Frida stood in a mud hole, pretending to be a weeping willow. She pointed to the treetop and shouted:

"Problims beware! Sundae's up there!"

Toot clapped and squealed. He puffed a #97.[5]

Sundae had kicked her sneakers off to climb the oak tree barefoot. (Sundae had especially grippy toes, which made tree climbing extra fun.) She was nearly to the top now. She blew a stray piece of blond hair away from her face as she stretched her arm long, reached up, and pulled herself to a higher branch. "You can stop digging, actually," she said brightly. "I did bury something down there seven years ago . . . but I just remembered that I moved it. I was afraid Ichabod would dig it up looking for truffles."

---

5 #97: Problim Malfunction: A toot used to insinuate someone is acting unusual, even by Problim standards. Smells like burned hair.

The pig *ork*ed as if offended by such a comment.

Sundae carefully swung to a thicker branch nearby and tossed an old metal lunch box down into Wendell's waiting arms.

Sal poked it with his trowel. "This is *not* the kind of treasure chest I pictured."

Frida leaped from the mudhole and twirled toward the treasure box, singing:

"Sundae's treasure in a box!
Sundae's treasure for a fox—WAAAH!"

Thea reached out and snatched Frida's arm just before she fell into the heart-shaped hole Sundae had dug earlier.

"Problims, pile up!" Sundae shouted as she jumped onto the ground.

The siblings plopped down in a tight circle, knees touching. Ichabod took his place beside Sal. And then Sundae took a particular kind of deep breath.

A storytelling breath.

"There's a deed inside this lunch box," Sundae began. "A deed for . . . a house!"

Sal held the box up to inspect it. "Well that's certainly convenient. And you're just now mentioning this? That you just happen to have buried a deed to a house?"

"It's not just any house," Sundae said. "It's the grand and glorious mansion belonging to . . ." She smiled sheepishly. "Frank Problim."

At the sound of this name, a heavy sadness settled over the Problim children.

Because the name Frank Problim made them feel all sorts of things:

sadness and joy,

and longing,

and even betrayal (just a little bit),

and a hollow kind of missing too;

that feeling most of all.

Wendell reached for his book and hugged it against his chest like a story-shield.

Thump, *bump*.

Thea leaned in a little closer to her twin.

Sal tossed his shovel down on the muddy ground. "Who cares about his dumb old house?"

"I do," Thea replied softly. "If it belonged to Grandpa, I care."

Wendell cared too. But the words were stuck in his throat, like they always were when he felt too much. Still, he nodded.

Grandpa. Mysterious and funny and kind and wild; gosh, he missed Grandpa Problim.

Sal glared at the lunch box as if it held a thousand biting wattabats. "I don't care about his house," Sal said. "I don't care about anything he has. Had, I mean."

Toot raised his eyebrows and popped a subtle #104.[6]

"Grandpa used to visit us sometimes, here in the swamp," Sal informed him. "But then he left without saying good-bye. He never came back. Why'd he give this to you, Sundae?"

Sundae shrugged. "Because I'm the oldest, maybe? He was frantic that last day and told me to hide this. To tell no one where it was. Not even Mom and Dad. 'When you come to an ending that surprises you,' he said, 'this will help you find a new beginning.' And it's happened, hasn't it? We definitely need a new beginning! Or a safe place to live, at least."

Safe. Thea liked that word. Wendell could feel her tension fizzling like soda bubbles.

---

6 #104: The Questioner: A fart demanding further explanation of a topic. Contains notes of spoiled milk and honeysuckle.

Sundae wrung her hands together as she concentrated. "Grandpa said this was a treasure, so it just seemed right to bury the whole thing. And I could tell by the look on his face that it mattered so much to him."

Toot puffed another #104, obviously wondering why Grandpa left.

Wendell wondered the same. Why *had* Grandpa left? He didn't know. His parents didn't talk about it. And why had Grandpa only visited *them*? Why did they never go visit Grandpa in his marvelous old mansion? Lost Cove wasn't *that* far away.

Before he could ask, Sundae said, "Mom and Dad wanted us raised here. And Grandpa agreed; there's no better place for creative thinkers than the Swampy Woods. We mind our own business! We solve our own problems! I always thought we wouldn't move on until our unschooling was complete." She shrugged. "But maybe it's time to move on now. Maybe Grandpa knew."

"Move on . . ." Sal drawled the words slowly. "You want to move into his house? In Lost Cove?"

Sundae beamed. "That's a great idea, Sal!"

"I wasn't suggesting it!" Sal shouted.

Sundae hugged the box close. "Grandpa Problim

was a good man, as wonderful as the best memory. He was an inventor, a storyteller, and a daring explorer. And he adored riddles! Imagine how fun his house will be! He was probably getting it ready just for us!"

Frida raised her hand and asked:

"When Grandpa Problim went away,
is the great forever where he stayed?"

"Heaven, you mean?" Sundae asked.

Frida nodded.

The children were silent. They looked to Sundae.

"Nobody knows," Sundae said sadly. "He disappeared on a daring adventure. He was knighted by the Queen of Andorra, just like Mom and Dad! Did you know that? Sir Frank Problim! He sent a few postcards, but then he . . . vanished."

Thea gasped softly. "How do people just vanish?"

Wendell didn't need to read her heart to know what she was thinking.

Was Grandpa's adventure similar to the perilous adventure their parents were on now?

Could they vanish too? Sevens were all around them, after all.

Thump, *bump. Try not to worry,* Wendell

heartspoke. And he reached for the box to try to change the topic. "Let's o-open it. It sounds like more than just a deed in th-there! He said treasure, right?" Wendell shook it fiercely. He pried at it with his fingernails.

"Just give it to Thea," Sal said. "She can open anything."

"I am good with locks," Thea said.

Safe in Thea's hands, the lid clicked open as gently as a music box. It was as if all she had to do was touch the thing—as if the box had been waiting for her.

The Problims crowded in close to see what was inside.

An old piece of paper—the deed, no doubt—lay on top of a pile of fabric. It was folded securely and curled at the edges. Sundae placed the paper in her lap and scanned the words. Then she reached in for the fabric—an old handkerchief, with some kind of long object inside it. She unwrapped it carefully.

Mona's eyes brightened. "Is that a bone? Was Grandfather Problim a *cannibal*?"

Toot puffed a #200.[7]

---

7 **#200:** The Toot of Intrigue: A faint, lingering aroma that helps Toot concentrate on unusual, yet enticing, bits of information. Smells like old books, cheese, and dust.

"It's not a bone, moron," Sal said, reaching for it. "It looks plantlike . . . but it's weirdly heavy."

The object looked a bit like a stick, Wendell thought. A bone-stick. It was the color of bone, at least. About as long as a pointer finger, with the width of a pencil. But the bone-stick had considerable weight to it. It had been severed at the edges, and it looked gold on the ends.

Thea carefully wrapped it back in the handkerchief. "It's important, if it's in there. We need to keep it safe." She reached in for the final item, a small pouch tied in a ribbon. Attached to the ribbon was a note:

For Sal,
A wise man who sets the world to blooming.

The chain pouring into Sal's hand held a tiny brass key.

"Does that mean anything to you?" Thea asked hopefully.

"Nope." Sal shrugged. "I'm telling you, Grandpa lost his mind there at the end. He probably didn't even mean to give it to me." Sal traced a finger gently over Grandpa Problim's handwriting. He shoved the chain into his pocket.

"Let's take all this with us to his house," Sundae said, putting the bone-stick back in the box and snapping it shut.

Toot patted Sundae's knee and puffed a #35.[8]

"Yes!" Sundae shouted. "Ears up, buttercups! Adventure is afoot! Let's head for Lost Cove!"

"Is anybody listening to me?" Sal asked them. "Lost Cove is a terrible place. Grandfather ran out on them seven years ago *for some reason*." He glared at Sundae. She beamed back at him.

"Sal," Sundae warned. This time her voice wasn't a happy chirp; it was filled with an edge her siblings rarely heard. Wendell glanced at his twin, to see if she'd noticed too. Thump, *bump*. Of course she had.

Sal and Sundae were keeping secrets.

"We're going," Sundae said, her voice firm but cheery. "There's no way to get in touch with Mom and Dad until I find a phone or internet. Or a very talented carrier pigeon. But here," she pointed to the metal box, "we have a deed . . ."

"And a booone," Mona cooed happily.

---

8 **#35:** The Fart of the Four Winds: The flatulent rally of a true adventure. Contains bold notes of dead fish in the ocean and chicken litter in a wide-open field.

"Problims! Let's play a game! Rummage through the rubble, collect everything that might be useful, anything we can take along with us! And, Wendell-Thea, you'll need to find some shoes."

"Maybe f-fear is like a wild onion blooming in the swamp," Wendell ruminated to his twin, as they skimmed the rubble for goods.

". . . huh?"

"M-maybe if you could peel back all these layers of your fear, and anxiety, and worry . . . you might f-find a good f-feeling too. Like exc-citement. I'm excited, deep down. Aren't you? Just a little bit?"

Thea shrugged. "I'm mostly just afraid."

Everyone is afraid of something, after all.

This was especially true in the town of Lost Cove.

Because the people there were still afraid of the same thing: the Problim family.

Seven Miles Away
(Is Far for a Squirrel)

The purple-tailed squirrel watched the Problim children from the prickly branches of an evergreen. Then the squirrel knew it was time to head out. (Sometimes people are afraid to have big adventures. But this is never, ever true of a squirrel.) The squirrel jumped. Airborne on a warm gust of wind, arms stretched wide, it landed with a soft thump a few trees down. And then it bounced from treetop to treetop, farther and farther away from the Swampy Woods.

Seven miles away, to be exact.

Lost Cove was a tiny nook of a town near the Carolina coastline, bordered by tall forests on two sides (full of excellent jumping trees!), and curved inward on the edge so the sea could cuddle close. A silver river used to snake around the town border, but the river had dried up years ago (for reasons no man or squirrel likes to talk about). Now all that was left was a rocky ravine, cutting through the land like a scar.

Soon the squirrel saw a familiar horizon ahead: a skyline zigzagged with church spires, old barns, and crumbling buildings (all fine places to rest if you're a rodent in need of a break). The streets in town were lined with old, pastel-colored homes now faded by the sun. A bakery called Good Donuts, run by a tattooed lady named Bertha, sat beside a bakery called Better Donuts, run by her sister, Dorothy. Today long lines stretched around both shops. Locals scuttled out each door with bags of baked goods and cups of steaming coffee, bumping into one another as they rushed up the hilly sidewalks.

The squirrel scampered along the ground unnoticed, dodging high-heeled boots and old sneakers as the crowd grew thicker—and the chatter grew louder. Main Street buzzed with activity today—just like it had years ago. The street used to be filled with grand Victorian houses (and even grander parties).

But most of those old homes had been razed. Now, almost every house on Main Street looked the same: boring mansions with swimming pools and perfectly manicured shrubs.

But two houses on Main Street looked different than all the others. And this is where the squirrel—and the rest of the chattering crowd—was headed. The squirrel jumped on the edge of a fountain in the middle of the street, and then onto the statue in the fountain's center. (The statue was a tribute to the brave adventurer Ponce de Léon—who had supposedly explored Lost Cove centuries ago. That was the town's only claim to fame. Well . . . that, plus the donuts.) The squirrel settled onto Ponce's shoulder and scanned the crowd.

House Number Five was probably the strangest house of all. Over the years, it had been remodeled and reshaped so much that nobody remembered its original form. In places it almost looked like a pirate ship, with planks extending from different windows and levels. Other parts of the house cantilevered over the yard of House Number Seven. It was as if Number Five was reaching for the house next door, trying to grab it or see what was inside.

But House Number Seven only looked sleepy and

old. The roof was a mess of flaky gray shingles. The house had been painted a lovely blue once, but now the paint chipped and peeled like dead skin. Boards covered the tall windows, to keep them from blowing out in the windy storms. The wrought-iron gate around the house was tall, locked, and overgrown with wild strands of ivy. The ivy was creeping up the front of the house now too—as if it were determined to keep it safe from everything about to happen.

After seven years vacant, House Number Seven was finally up for auction.

And there was one woman in the town of Lost Cove who was determined to have it. No one really doubted she would get it. She was already waiting to bid, of course. She'd been near the gate for hours, watching the crowd gather from behind dark, oversized sunglasses. Her lips held the tiniest hint of a smile. Not a kind smile, though.

The squirrel narrowed its eyes at her.

Squirrels always know a villain when they see one.

Desdemona

Desdemona O'Pinion pushed her sunglasses up higher on her nose and tapped her long red fingernails together. An unseasonal chilly wind had blown in from the sea, ruffling her hair. The air today felt cold and wet and perfect for house smashing.

Not that she planned to smash it . . . yet. First she wanted to get inside it. Explore for a while. Find what she was looking for. What she'd always been looking for: a map. One that would lead the way to riches untold. Desdemona would find it.

Then she'd wreck the place. Every last trace of it.

Ten more minutes and that wretched piece of property would be hers.

After all these years . . .

"Can we go now, Mom?" Desdemona's daughter, Carley-Rue, sighed and fidgeted and groaned. Carley-Rue, age ten, had been the reigning princess of the Little Miss Lost Cove Corn Dog Festival for the past three years. She wore her tiara and sash everywhere she went—to school, to church, to take her cat for walks. (Carley-Rue's cat, Miss Florida 1987, was a rare Himalayan Adventuring Cat.)

It never hurts to remind people that you are important, Desdemona would say when Carley-Rue complained about the itchy crown. It's why Desdemona had insisted on keeping her maiden name: O'Pinion! And why she insisted her children did as well. O'Pinion was a name that meant power. As if anyone in town could forget the O'Pinions were important. They owned everything they wanted. (And they wanted almost everything.)

Desdemona rested her hands on her daughter's shoulders. Firmly. "No more grumbling, Rue Baby. We're about to own this big, ugly eyesore of a house. And then you know what we'll do?" Desdemona smiled sweetly. "We'll pull this place apart, board by board, brick by brick, and see what's inside it!"

Lightning bolts of excitement zinged inside

Desdemona's chest as she looked up at the old mansion. "There's no house in the world like this one."

Desdemona's teenage son, Will, stood beside his sister with a CosmicMorpho 3030 Mask covering his eyes. Unfortunately, the internet connection was terrible outside, so he kept yanking his head trying to get the mask to work. "Ugh, Mom! I'm going back to my room."

"Not yet. I want us all to be here to witness this moment. Why don't you take that thing off so you can see?"

Will pushed his mask into his hair and groaned. "What's to see? It's the same old house next door." And then he raised his eyebrows as seven sleek black SUVs pulled onto the street and stopped.

Carley-Rue fluffed her hair. "Is the president coming to see us smash the house?"

"Read what the cars say, idiot," Will told her. "They're from something called . . . the Society for the Protection of Unwanted Children."

"They might not be necessary," Desdemona said, patting Carley-Rue's shoulder. "I like to think of them as . . . insurance. Just in case anything funny happens today."

She had no time for funny, after all.

She only had time for wonderful.

She'd build a private clubhouse on that lot, complete with a lagoon-style swimming pool, a bocce ball court, and a private latte station. Soon . . . SOON. That word had never sounded so lovely. She almost laughed out loud just thinking about it.

The steady buzz of chatter grew louder as the mayor of Lost Cove parked his old Ford pickup in the street, behind the SUVs. He made his way toward the gate surrounding Number Seven Main Street, shaking hands with a few folks as he passed by. "G'morning, friends." He nodded to the gathering crowd. He tucked his thumbs into the pockets of his jeans and looked down. Mayor Wordhouse was a small, scrawny man with wiry white hair. He always wore jeans, a plaid shirt, and suspenders, even for very important functions like this. Desdemona found this attire highly inappropriate. "I must admit . . . my heart's heavy as a sack of cement this morning. I feel that we should take a moment, before this place is auctioned, to remember how special it used to be."

Desdemona snorted. "No need to be sentimental. Joffkins! What time is it?"

Her brother, Joffkins, startled. He checked his shiny watch, which had been outfitted with a compass, a weight scale, and all sorts of other equipment he'd need for an adventure hike. (Not that he'd ever actually been hiking.)

"Ten till," he said as he smoothed his graying hair behind his ears. He reached out to pat his older sister's shoulder, but she shrugged away. "Why so tense, Desdemona?"

"No reason," she mumbled, glancing down the street. Surely the Problems didn't have any last tricks up their dirty sleeves . . .

"Now, I know some of you are in a big ol' hurry," the mayor said, raising a fuzzy white eyebrow in Desdemona's direction. "I'm all for innovation. But I'll be honest—it pains my soul when people decide to smash down every reminder we have of the past. This place especially. I remember the parties they used to have in this yard, barefoot dances under paper-star lanterns . . ."

"So uncivilized," Desdemona mumbled.

"Those were good days," the mayor continued. "Before this old house is gone, I'd like to give it a proper good-bye. This home was something special. Losing it feels a little bit like saying farewell to an old friend. So let's take a minute, now. And remember something we loved."

Everyone hushed their whispering and stilled their moving. Soft sounds of summer filled the air: Crickets singing. Bull frogs *yerrrp*-ing. A low hum of wattabat wings from the general direction of the Swampy Woods. Somewhere far off, a motor revved. A cell phone jingled in someone's pocket. And as always, there was that faithful *shh* of the nearby sea.

"Why won't he get on with it?" Desdemona asked.

Joffkins leaned over and whispered, "Only eight more minutes."

Desdemona glared at the mayor, who stood with his head bowed, hat over his heart. She'd never had any difficulty intimidating most people—with her words, her stare, her money, her height. Something always worked. And the mayor was such a scrawny, soft-spoken man. That's why she'd voted for him; because he'd surely do anything she wanted. But he rarely seemed intimidated by her in the least. Which was frustrating.

The mayor looked over the crowd. "Anybody have any words they'd like to say? In memory of this house?"

As if a house were a person. As if a house could tell a story. Well . . . that house did have a story.

A terrible one. The sooner it was erased from the town's map, the better they all would be.

No one spoke.

But everyone began to . . . sniff.

"Whoa," Mary Wong fanned the air in front of her nose dramatically. "What is that smell? Desdemona, is that your new perfume?"

Desdemona raised her eyebrows. "Excuse me?"

"Wait, no. That's not perfume," Mrs. Wong said, her nose wrinkling in disgust. She jostled the shoulder of her son, Noah. "Did you toot?" she asked through clenched teeth.

"No!" he said. And then he too took a deep breath. And laughed. "Gross!"

Bertha Martin stood with her hands on her hips, the sleeves of her Good Donuts T-shirt rolled back to show her flag tattoo. She sniffed. Nodded. "Oh shoot, yeah. That's a fierce fart, is what that is." She glanced over at her sister, Dorothy. Gave her a thumbs-up.

"It wasn't me!" Dorothy chimed in. "I'd claim it. I've got no scruples."

Suddenly the mayor's speech was drowned out by a rising chorus of whispers. And then gasps.

There is a sound unique to small towns like Lost

Cove, more common than the rise and fall of the cricket song or a wild cicada concert in the heat of a summer night. Rumors have a rhythm, you see: like a hiss and a rattle and a chorus of snakes.

Someone was coming.

Some "ones," more like.

Desdemona glared at the edge of the street. "They're here." She seethed. And then she grinned. "Good."

Return of the Seven

Thea and Wendell concentrated on steering their bicycle built for two down Main Street without wrecking. The front wheel was bent, so the bike swiveled as it *rickity-thumped* over the cobblestone road. Mostly because Frida insisted on sitting in the front basket, playing her ukulele.

"Do you see all the people around that house?" Thea asked. "What if there was an accident? What if somebody is hurt?"

"Dear God in heaven," Thea heard an elderly lady say. "It's *them*."

"No one is hurt!" Sundae beamed. "It's a welcome party!"

Sundae led the Problim parade, pulling a large wagon full of precious junk that the Problims had managed to salvage from their home: books, blankets, a few stuffed animals, a brass lamp that looked like a rabbit, a top hat, and a box of cereal. She waved happily at the crowd. Though sweaty and covered in dust, her smile was still as bright as a July sunrise.

Ichabod marched beside Sundae's wagon, snout tipped up. Atop the pig sat Toot Problim, his chin high and proud. He snuggled a dirty teddy bear close to his heart. The second wave of Toot's #58[9] wafted toward the crowd and caused some of the women to totter in their high heels.

"Hello, hello! Good morning!" Sundae called out, her blond ponytail swishing behind her. "We're your new neighbors!"

Toot carried the deed in his chubby fist. He hoisted it up proudly, like a tiny king, for all to see.

Thea noticed something odd: as the Problims moved closer, the adults began to back away . . . but just far enough that they could still get a look

---

9 **#58**: The Roving Wanderer: Happens when in transit. Smells like roadkill.

at them. Thea knew her family looked dirty. They were still covered in chalky debris, after all. But that didn't seem so bad, considering they'd survived an explosion.

"That boy . . . ," said a woman with dark hair and a chunky blue necklace. She pulled her son back hard against her chest. "That child has blades on his arms!"

"Gardening tools," Sal mumbled.

A little girl's eyes widened as she saw Ichabod. "Ew. That is a pig. There are no pigs allowed on Main Street . . . are there, Mommy?"

Frida sang:

"We have a fox,
We have a swine,
Oh friends, this is our time to shine!"

She jumped out of the basket, did a quick stretch, and then ran full force at the crowd.

"Go, Frida, go!" Sundae squealed.

"What's a Frida?" someone mumbled.

The fox pumped her arms. She yelled:

"I shall not blink, I shall not slip!
Make way, make way! The fox must flip!"

Frida cartwheeled into the crowd, accidentally crashing into Will O'Pinion. Who crashed into Carley-Rue, who fell into Mrs. Wong. And then the crowd became human dominoes falling to the ground. Frida jumped up and raised her arms in victory. Toot (born on a Tuesday, and always full of grace) scrambled down from the pig. He waddled around trying to help people stand, which is difficult when your arms are tiny.

Last in line, Mona swiveled her pink scooter to a stop. She opened her black umbrella to shield her precious plant.

Carley-Rue's crown sat sideways on her head as she stood and eyed them carefully. "Mommy . . . are those the . . ."

"Shush!" Desdemona pressed her hand over Carley-Rue's mouth. "Who cares? Onward, Mayor!" And then more quietly, she added, "This place is mine."

"This place is ours, actually," Sundae announced brightly. She made her way through the crowd and presented the mayor with the deed. "Hello, my fellow Covians. Thank you so much for gathering to greet us! I'm not sure how the word got out, but I'm so tickled to meet you."

The mayor smiled and raised a fuzzy eyebrow. "And you are?"

"Sundae," she said brightly. And then she pulled her shoulders back and proudly declared, "Sundae Problim."

The crowd gasped and fell completely silent. Problim.

Desdemona clenched her fists.

"No way," Noah gasped. "We thought you were legends! We dress up like you guys for Halloween!"

Bertha rubbed her hands together. "Now this is getting interesting . . ."

"The Problims . . . ," someone whispered. "That family had magic. Bad magic . . ."

A sputtery *whooosh* sound filled the air. The crowd looked to Toot.

"That's #124[10]," Sundae clarified for everyone. "Happens when he's excited. And we are all thrilled to be your neighbors. We would love to get settled in to our house and—"

"YOUR house?" Desdemona shouted. The Problim children all spun to look at her.

---

10 **#124:** The Joyful, Joyful: Simple flatulence of happiness. Smells like a week-old bouquet of daisies.

"Mom." Will pulled his phone off his eyes. "Chill."

"I don't chill!"

"Let's all keep calm now," the mayor declared. He pulled his glasses from his front pocket and read the deed Sundae handed over. As he read, the crowd pushed in closer.

"This does appear to be legitimate." The mayor nodded and turned his attention to the people of Lost Cove. "This is the deed for the house of Frank Problim, leaving this home to his children and their children . . ."

Desdemona clutched her brother's arm, digging her nails deep into his skin until he pulled away with an "Ouch!"

She stepped closer, so Sundae could see her own reflection in the woman's sunglasses. They reminded Sundae of bug eyes. Of a large spider. Not spiders like the ones Wendell and Thea raised that liked to cuddle and do circus tricks. More like the spiders that built fine, invisible webs on the porch of the bungalow to trap summer fireflies.

"But how do we know you are Problims, with an *i*, and not just PROBLEMS?" Desdemona asked, her fingers still curved like claws. "Where *are* your parents? You can't deed a house to a child, Mayor. She can't be more than ten!"

Sundae answered thoughtfully, "Actually, I'm a space-efficient sixteen! My parents are archeologists on a secret mission for the Queen of Andorra. So I take care of my siblings. We take care of one another, actually."

"At least there are only six of them," someone said softly. "Six are easy to deal with. It's when it's seven that bad things happen."

Desdemona and Joffkins both shivered at some distant memory.

"Actually, there are seven of us," Sundae added sheepishly.

"They're lying anyway," Desdemona said. "Do you know what happens to children who lie?"

Toot shook his head.

"Oh, babies. Foolish babies. Terrible things happen to children who don't tell the truth. They're separated. They're taken far, far away from one another. Let's see . . . seven children. Seven continents. Seven beautiful cars to take you all away from one another. That'd fit, wouldn't it?" The hint of a grin twitched at the corners of Desdemona's mouth.

Thea looked around at the terrified faces of the

townspeople. "But we aren't lying."

"But you are," Desdemona said. "Because the real Problems moved far away from this town many years ago. Don't worry, Mayor. I was prepared for this."

Desdemona snapped and waved to the black SUVs. Men and women in wrinkly black suits jumped out, eyes locked on the Problems.

Desdemona grinned. "I heard there were terrible miscreants living out in the Swampy Woods; stealing other peoples' identities, wreaking havoc on every acre of nature they touch. To keep my children safe, I formed the Society for the Protection of Unwanted Children—"

Sal raised an eyebrow. "That's seriously what it's called?"

"Yes!" Desdemona continued, "They are trained and ready to make sure none of our children are in danger. Separate them."

Thea felt paralyzed by her fear. Wendell grabbed her and yanked her into the tight circle of dirty siblings, all behind Sundae. As if Sundae—tiny, obnoxiously happy Sundae—could protect them from this terrible twist of events. "Whoa there, friends!" Sundae said, smiling at the people in dark suits. "Back off. I'm serious! This is all perfectly legal!"

"That's true," said the mayor as he scanned the deed. "If you are the Problim children, you can live here. And I believe you are, but we need documentation, see."

"Of course!" Sundae nodded. "I'll find our birth certificates . . . or something. And I'll try to call our parents once we're settled in." (The paperwork was buried somewhere in the bungalow rubble, so Sundae hoped they didn't ask to see it. But it did technically exist.) "They'll be back soon anyway."

"When exactly?" Desdemona demanded.

"Within a month," Sundae said. "Or two. They'll be here lickety-split!" Sundae returned her attention to the mayor. He seemed far more reasonable than the lady with the big sunglasses. "I understand we'll have to prove our identity somehow. But due to unforeseen circumstances, we need to move in right away."

"Of course," the mayor assured her. He even offered her a kind half smile.

Desdemona glared at him from behind her shades. "Do you remember what happened the last time Problims were in this town, Mayor?"

"Now, Desdemona . . ."

"I agree with Desdemona!" shouted a blond lady. "They're probably thieves trying to swindle us. And if they are Problims . . . that's even worse! This neighborhood has been blessedly Problim-free for years. I won't stand for it. They can't stay."

"Agreed," someone shouted.

"Me too!" came the voice of a burly man in the back of the crowd.

"Let's vote on it!" yelled Carley-Rue.

Sundae and her siblings looked thoroughly confused.

Thea's heart felt cold. Wendell shivered at the chill. How could people hate you who barely even knew you? And what could they possibly hate?

Thea looked at her siblings—her marvelous, wonderful, wild-fun siblings. Midge Lodestar said that sometimes it was hard to make friends because people are shy. But it never occurred to Thea that people wouldn't want to be her friend just because of her family.

The mayor held up his hands again. "People! That's enough. These are kids here, see? I believe these are Frank Problim's grandkids. And we shouldn't hold them responsible for the grief their grandpa caused this town."

"I remember the day he nearly made Stan O'Pinion walk the plank up there." Dorothy pointed to the roof of House Number Five. She shivered. "That feud started out funny, but it turned into something . . . terrible."

"Enough," the mayor pleaded. "Please. Now, Miss Sundae, I'm obliged to let you stay in this place—" The crowd grumbled angrily.

"PROVIDED," the mayor said more loudly to quiet them down, "that you bring me proof that you are the Problim children. I'm talking birth certificates. Or your parents showing up. You've got twenty-one days to show me some identification, okay? That's the law too, you see."

Thea's heart shivered at the number. Twenty-one days. Three sevens. She glanced at her twin. Sweat already beaded on Wendell's forehead. The sevens were still piling up, and that meant trouble was still headed their way.

The mayor handed Sundae a large skeleton key, and he glared at the Society for the Protection of Unwanted Children. "We won't be needing your services today."

Sundae cleared her throat, looking around at the

quiet, stunned crowd and giving them her widest, brightest smile. "We're so looking forward to being your neighbors."

Then she motioned for her siblings to follow her. None of the neighbors moved. None except Desdemona—who sauntered catlike beside the children all the way to the gate, in the perfect position to glare at Sundae Problim as the girl pushed the key into the lock.

Sundae lifted her chin proudly and smiled.

Sundae wasn't distrusting in general. But she certainly didn't trust the spider woman. And she wanted her to know that she was not afraid of her. Not for a second.

The squirrel pounced up into the tallest tree to get a good look at the house next door—House Number Five.

The house of Desdemona O'Pinion.

This house was lived in, but you wouldn't know it. Rooms were mostly dark. Thick curtains stayed drawn to keep the paintings on the walls from fading. Dust motes floated through the occasional beam of sunlight that snuck in through the draperies. And the light did find a way in that day.

Because one person who lived in a secluded suite in that lonesome old house was very interested in the commotion next door. He'd pulled back the curtain to watch the show. But he'd never planned on such a spectacle.

His hand, old and bent, covered by age spots and bubbled by blue veins, trembled with happiness as it held back the dusty curtain. A strange feeling—between fear and excitement—filled this man's heart when he saw the children disappear behind the old gate of Number Seven.

"Until the seven do return," he whispered with a smile in his voice. He chuckled softly and closed the curtain.

Sir Frank's
Marvelous Mansion

The sound of the rusty key clicking inside the lock gave Thea's heart a happy thrill. She'd liked keys and locks since she was a baby, the same way some kids like rattles and teddy bears. She used to chain up Wendell just to see what she could use to pick the lock: pins, sticks, even a toothpick would work. Locks were easy.

"Oh, just let me do it!" Thea said anxiously. "We need to get inside. Maybe Grandpa has copies of our birth certificates or pictures of us—something!"

"But locked doors are fun!" Sundae said.

"Here's what's not fun," Sal offered. "The weirdos in this town. What kind of town forms a society for unwanted children?"

Wendell nodded. "And did you h-hear that one lady ask about the f-feud? What's that?"

Thump, *bump*. "And magic," Thea said softly. "Did you hear them say our family was magic?" Most of the children, plus the pig, all nodded.

"Grandpa wasn't magic," Sal said. "He lost his mind. Exhibit A: he told Sundae to bury a stick and a key in the yard. Exhibit B: that funny little porch on the roof up there. Look at that thing! It could fall down at any minute. I hereby name it the Porch of Certain Death." Sal grinned. "I bet if we got a rope around those gargoyles on either side, we could climb it! Let's race to the top!"

Thea scowled. "Before or after the Society for the Protection of Unwanted Children rounds us up and sends us to seven different continents? That woman wasn't joking, Sal. She meant what she said. Here, let me try the lock . . ."

Thea barely jiggled the key, and it opened with a long, slow squeak.

Together, the Problim children ran through the front door and into the darkness of Frank's old Victorian. The air inside the house was humid and musty.

"As soon as we can see," Sundae said as she staggered around, bumping into her siblings, "we're looking for birth certificates, pictures, proof—Problim proof!"

"The s-smell reminds me of the library in the bungalow," Wendell said.

Thea liked that thought. Maybe this house was full of dusty dreams and old stories too. If a place was full of books and family and animals, Thea knew she could feel home there. If they got to stay there. If they didn't get sent away.

Sal pulled a flashlight from his tool belt, but Mona pushed past him before he could turn it on.

"I can see perfectly well in the dark, thank you very much. Let me lead the way." (Mona's night vision was legendary in the Problim family. It was part of what made her such a formidable foe.)

"Nope." Sal shoved his way to the front. "If you lead, we'll end up locked in the basement. *I* will lead."

"Terrible idea," Mona said softly.

And then came the gentle, rancid odor of a #165.[11]

------

11 **#165**: The Propanetankerous: Smells a bit like a gas leak, but more subtle and refined. Means: PAY ATTENTION TO ME.

Thea reached down, pulling Toot into her arms. "He's pointing to those tall windows. If we could get those boards off, think of how much light we'd have!"

The windows framed the front door, and both were covered in boards. Only slats of light managed to creep through. Sal pulled a crowbar from his left sleeve and worked the low board loose. Then the next one. Thea gasped as the room was illuminated. The foyer reminded her of a cathedral she'd seen in one of Wendell's books. Wendell was remembering the same picture as he squinted, his gaze drifting higher and higher.

As the sun passed over the house, the Problim children noticed a large, circular, stained-glass window near the ceiling. The window was partially boarded too. But it looked to be patterned like pie pieces, each piece with a colorful symbol.

"I'll have to get the rappelling gear to move those," Sal said.

"I'll h-help you." Wendell couldn't wait to see the pattern hidden there. Looking up at the window was like being inside a kaleidoscope, as it filtered down pieces of rainbow light all over their faces. Wendell lifted his arms and imagined the light like water.

Running, dripping, shining through his hands.

"Here's the staircase!" Thea jogged up a few steps. "Look how it swirls! It spirals all the way to the top of the house!"

"And hopscotch floors!" Frida shouted as she jumped crisscross over the black-and-white checkered marble.

"Square to square
and covered in dust!
Adventure we shall!
Adventure we mu—"

Frida slid in the dust and knocked against the statue of a silver-armored soldier at the base of the stairs, which fell into a clattery heap on the floor. (Frida was a tiny Problim, but she had all the force of a bowling ball.) Toot scrambled down from Wendell's arms and waddled over to pick up the knight. Sundae assisted him.

"You'd think our parents would have told us about this place . . . ," Thea said in awe, stepping over the soldier. "Or that Grandpa would have brought us here to visit."

"Stay on task!" Sundae declared. "Let's search for Problim proof!"

The Problim children scrambled. The house would take a long time to search, because it was bigger than the Problims were used to. Thea and Wendell explored the downstairs rooms, which all had soft-purple walls.

"Grandpa loved the color p-purple," Wendell said as he rummaged through an old trunk. "He wore that old purple velvet jacket all the time. He looked like a grand old magician when he came to visit. Do you r-remember?"

"Yes." Thea breathed as she pulled a pale-purple blanket from the drawer of an antique dresser. And then she remembered the swoosh of the purple squirrel they'd seen scampering around the swamp that morning. "Wendell, do you think the robo-squirrel was a—"

"A s-sign?" Wendell finished excitedly.

"Maybe?"

"Maybe!"

Thump, *bump*.

Thea believed in signs. Wendell believed in wonders. He'd always felt sorry for people who didn't believe in miracles. How could anybody live in such a weirdly wonderful world and not see magic tangled inside it?

Maybe sevens were a good thing.

Maybe, just maybe, the Problims were in Lost Cove for a reason.

⁓

And yet, after hours of searching, the Problim children found no proof.

Downstairs, they discovered a sitting room full of furniture covered in sheets, a kitchen (which wasn't functional yet), and a dining room with a long table, which was painted with a map of the world. They also found a library.

As the board came loose from the library window, light flooded the room—reaching immediately for the spines of hundreds of books shelved on the far wall.

"This . . ." Wendell sighed as he looked over the shelves. "Th-this is the most b-beautiful place I've ever seen."

"And look here," Thea said as she walked closer to the statue of a girl holding a lantern. "She looks so brave, doesn't she? Hello, Statue. Can you tell me where to find proof of my relation to Frank Problim?"

The statue was only as tall as Sundae, and caked in dust. Thea wiped the dirt from the statue's face. Then she dusted the lantern the girl was holding. The lantern was made of mirror pieces, and as Thea wiped off the grime, the sunlight sparkled against the glass, making a rainbow path across the room. Frida turned a cartwheel, landed on the rainbow path, and began to tiptoe across it as if it were a balance beam.

A brass nameplate was attached to the base of the statue:

> **THEODORA PROBLIM**
> She was never afraid of Far-to-Go

"Sal!" Thea gasped. "She had to be a relative. Do you think she was a Thursday, like me?"

"Maybe," Sal said, shielding his eyes from the rainbow beam of light. "Could you push Theodora Problim in the corner, though? These rainbows are giving me a happiness headache."

A large clock on the library wall made a drumbeat

ticking sound as the Problims explored the room. But it didn't tick menacingly, like some clocks do:

Time's up.
  Time's up.
    Time's up.

No, this clock had a sweeter sound, Thea thought. More like a steady heartbeat.

Time is short.
  Time is sweet.
    Live it well.

"Look here," Sundae said as she pulled a sheet from the painting on one of the library walls.

Grandpa Problim riding a unicorn.

Another painting showed Grandma Problim sliding down a rainbow.

And then—a painting of seven children. They had mud-smudged faces and bright eyes. The girls wore braids. The boys wore hats and bandannas and sideways grins.

"That littlest one might be Grandpa Problim," Sundae said, pointing to the smallest boy in the group. "Dad said Grandpa was born with white hair, like he was always meant to be a wise old soul. And he was one of seven—like all of us."

"Really?" Thea exclaimed, running closer to the painting. "I'll bet Theodora Problim was his sister! I never knew he was a seven!"

"There's a lot you don't know," Sal mumbled.

Sundae cleared her throat. "Sal just means that sevens run in our family, I think. Every other generation or so . . . seems to have a group of seven . . ."

"What's that Grandpa is holding?" Sal asked. He climbed on Wendell's shoulders so he could see more closely.

Thea squinted at the object in Grandpa's hand. Was it some kind of scepter? Or fishing rod? Or . . .

"Wait a sec . . ." Sal stepped closer. "That stick looks like a really big version of the bone-stick he gave us. Look! It has the gold rings all the way down."

Thea's wild heart thundered. "Grandpa wanted us to be here," Thea said. "I know it. Maybe there's a bigger version of this stick somewhere! Maybe he wanted us to do something with it!"

"With a *stick*?" Sal said, climbing down from his brother's shoulders. "Some treasure."

"You guys! Come quick!" Frida trilled:

"Come look and see!
The stairs become a slide!
Pull the lever, take a leap!
And hang on for the ride!"

Wendell ran out into the hall in time to see Frida slide down onto the floor, screaming happily. Ichabod was up next. He waddled to the top of the slide and jumped, gliding down on his tummy. *Ork-ork-ork!* He slid onto the floor and bounced around, wiggling his curly tail. For a while, they took turns zooming down.

After several slides, plus some upstairs exploration, the Problems came to two conclusions.

One: Grandpa's house was awesome.

Two: there was absolutely no proof whatsoever that they were related to him.

"We'll f-figure something out," Wendell assured Thea. "It can't be that h-hard to prove. Maybe we could buy a little time, though . . . if we kn-knew why people were so afraid of us . . ."

Thea continued, "And why they don't want us in their town . . ."

"Or what in the world they were t-talking about—the feud, the magic, all that s-stuff . . ."

"Then they might let us stay until Mom and Dad come home," Thea said. "Even if we don't have proof." She tried to swallow down the fear stuck in her throat. But all she could imagine were those sleek SUVs, all seven of them, waiting to carry her away from her siblings.

"I know!" Wendell shouted. "We need circus s-spiders! They could help."

Thea's eyes twinkled. "Of course they could!"

Wendell beamed. "I'll tell Mona to go get them. Creepy creatures love Mona."

Thump, *bump*. Twins for the win!

That night, Sal turned on the power.

("Electricity is easy," he said.)

And Wendell configured all the water pipes. ("Water is easy," he said.) Wendell had just wiped layers of dust off the counters and pulled together enough ingredients to make pancakes when his twin sister called for him.

"Wendell!"

He found her standing in front of the library bookshelf, with a wide-eyed, startled look on her face. The bookshelf had moved a few feet away from the wall to reveal a tunnel. "There's a squirrel statue on the shelf," she told him. "Like the robo-squirrel in the woods. So I reached to touch it and the whole shelf moved!"

"A s-secret passage!"

The tunnel surged upward, full of stairs that were easy to trip over. Eventually the passage narrowed, and Wendell felt around the wall until his hand passed over another lever. With a pull, a door popped open. They ran through at the same time, into a round room full of painted stars. A large window looked out over the town. The walls around that window were sky blue, rising to a navy-colored ceiling freckled by shining wonders. Stars sparkled. Comets soared. Someone had painted a fizzy-bright Milky Way and a rocket rising into the abyss.

Wendell wandered to the window and looked out over the neighborhood. Main Street was full of homes, but he could see plenty of houses beyond that too. "Come look, Th-Thea."

"I'm afraid of heights," she reminded him. "Most of all. More than anything." She'd had a zillion nightmares about falling. That was another reason she slept on the ground, which he should have known. "I think I'm allergic to gravity."

"Just stand close, then. Look, there's Ponce de León. And you can see so many houses . . . Can you imagine how many f-friends we could make here?"

"*If* they don't send us to seven different continents." Thea moved carefully toward the window. She didn't get as close as Wendell. But she was tall enough to be able to see the view, even from a distance. "Midge Lodestar says there's nothing in the world like a true-blue friend. Plus, friends eat free on Taco Tuesday. Whatever that means."

"But they didn't act very f-friendly earlier. They acted afraid of us."

Thea gulped. "I was afraid of them, too."

"Never fear! The fox is here!" came a sweet voice from the tunnel.

"Whoa!" Sal's voice echoed. "They found a secret passage!"

But before their siblings could join them in the room of stars, Toot puffed a #2.[12]

Frida bounced into the room:

---

12 **#2: The Hangry Puff:** A warning Toot fires to remind his family that if he doesn't eat soon his mood will quickly sour. Smells like takeout food forgotten in a car overnight.

"The baby flatulates,
The fox translates:
Refuse to feed the baby, and lo
A mighty tantrum he will throw!"

"I'll come down and f-finish dinner," Wendell said.

"Wendell, we should build our bunks here! In the Room of Constellations!"

"You c-can," Wendell pushed his glasses up on his nose. "But I want to bunk in the l-library."

"But . . . we always bunk in the same room."

"Wendell! Thea!" Sundae called from down below. "Come on! Pancake party!"

Wendell chewed on his lip as he considered something. "Have you n-noticed we're always Wendell-Thea? Like one p-person? Does that ever bother you at all?"

"No!" she answered quickly. "Why should it?"

"No reason," he mumbled as he disappeared into the tunnel.

Thea spun slowly, taking in the starry walls of the hidden space place.

"Why did you bring us here?" she whispered as if the room would talk to her. Although that would have been super creepy if it had. Thankfully, it didn't. The only response Thea heard was the chatter and clatter of her siblings trying to find food downstairs. She finally left to join them.

However, if she'd lingered and listened just a bit more closely, she might have heard the sound of a slow music box. In the tall magnolia tree beside the window, the purple-tailed squirrel waited. Its tail swished. The music played.

The tall oaks on Main Street shivered with excitement. And so did the house itself.

A brass rabbit on the library shelf twitched its mechanical ears.

A robotic phoenix in the corner of the sitting room lifted its wing, and its gold feathers dangled and jingled like bells.

Soon

    Soon

        Soon . . . ticked the big clock in the downstairs room.

House Number Seven was waking up again, finally, after so many years asleep.

A Petition for Removal

For a week, nobody saw the Problim children. And folks in Lost Cove began to wonder if, maybe, the children really were Frank Problim's kinfolk and maybe not as bad or dangerous as their grandfather had been. So Desdemona O'Pinion did her part to call each lady in the Mansion Owners Observation Society (MOOS, for short) and remind them of all the havoc the Problim family had caused so many years ago.

Then came Saturday morning.

The residents of Main Street in Lost Cove woke to fog.

Thick, hideous, soupy fog.

It was the most horribly exciting thing that had happened on Main Street in ages.

Mrs. Timberwhiff noticed it first, when she walked to get the morning paper that she never actually took out of the wrapper. Mist in the Cove normally settled over Main Street like a lovely layer of gossamer. They used the picture in brochures, even. To lure the right kind of new families to the neighborhood. But this fog was so thick it might be dangerous. Worst of all, it was ugly.

"I'll call Desdemona about this," Mrs. Timberwhiff huffed. Because if anybody could tell the weather what to do, it was certainly Desdemona O'Pinion, founder and president of MOOS.

Mrs. Timberwhiff wasn't the only neighbor who called Desdemona that morning. Desdemona's phone began buzzing and ringing nonstop, interrupting her morning meditation. She finally stomped out of the house wearing her pajamas and a blue fluffy bathrobe. She immediately began coughing, trying to swat the fog away as if it were a hefty billow of smoke.

From her front yard, she could see exactly where it came from—as if she'd had any doubt.

The fog was coming from Number Seven. Of

course. Fog wrapped around that old Victorian trash heap like a cloudy scarf. By noon, only the tall tower—the one with the rickety porch wrapped around it—was visible. Plus, Desdemona could hear things inside the fog: hammering, laughing, something that sounded like a saw. Desdemona grabbed a pair of binoculars and crawled to the edge of one of the planks extended from the windows of her home. But no matter how hard she looked, she couldn't see through the mist.

Bertha came running down the street. Bertha was seventy years old, and she had just run her seventh marathon. Desdemona knew there was no avoiding her. "Dezi! There you are!"

Desdemona flinched. She hated it when people called her Dezi, as if she were still ten years old.

"Dez! Dezi!"

"I hear you, Bertha," she said with a forced smile.

"That wild fog! It's coming from Number Seven, yeah? Everybody at the bakeries are talking about those kiddos."

"Not for long," Desdemona said.

Dorothy came riding up next in a golf cart. "Are y'all talking about the Problim children?"

"Yep!" Bertha said. "I'm here to tell you now,

the Problims have always been . . . touched. Touched with some dark magic, I believe."

Desdemona groaned. "They're not magic."

But Bertha carried on. "I'm old enough to remember when Frank's family lived here, you know. He had a bunch of siblings too. They lost one in the war, and some moved away. But ohhh, I remember. When Frank Problim and his wild bunch of siblings got together, strange things started happening. But when Frank only had one son—well—we thought all the strangeness was over."

Desdemona tried to interject, but Bertha was on a roll. "And that was all before the Great Feud. Before Frank Problim went mad. And now, six children, dirty as swamp rats, come back to claim their granddaddy's estate . . ."

"Seven," Desdemona corrected with a shiver. "The oldest one said there were seven children. But they won't be here long."

Noah Wong arrived next, pushing a double stroller. One side held his baby sister, a toddler too busy napping to notice the fog. The other side contained the family's Himalayan Adventuring Cat, licking her paws nonchalantly as she reclined. (Once Desdemona bought a Himalayan Adventuring Cat for Carley-Rue, every family in the neighborhood had to have one.) "Somebody told my mom that they've seen the one with the blades walking around at night." Noah spoke low, as if he was afraid that Sal would overhear. "Isn't that cool?"

"No, not cool," Desdemona scolded. "All of you children are in danger as long as they're here. In fact," Desdemona said, her audience of terrified moms now primed, "if we get enough signatures on a petition for removal, the Society for the Protection of Unwanted Children would come see what's going on. And find out if they really have guardians. And if they don't, they could find safe homes for them. Far, far away from here."

Everyone nodded enthusiastically. Of course Desdemona had come up with the perfect plan.

"Honestly, I'd forgotten all about the Problim family," someone said. "What was the name of Frank's son, Desdemona? Wasn't he your age?"

"Major." Desdemona seethed. "Major Problim."

Oh yes, she would be happy to get that petition circulating. She'd start it this afternoon.

"Shh!" Bertha hissed. "Listen! Do y'all hear that?"

Mingled with the early morning breeze, a soft whistle floated down Main Street.

The crowd inched closer to one another, all straining their necks and standing on their toes watching toward the end of the lane. At last, the silhouette of a girl on a scooter emerged from the fog. The wheels made a *poppity* rolling sound over the cobblestones. The rider wore a pink dress and a black sweater. Her black hair rippled freely in the breeze. Her umbrella was folded into a basket on the front, alongside a Venus flytrap in a pink pot.

"That's the pretty one," Carley-Rue growled.

"Have you ever seen such a beautiful child?" Mrs. Timberwhiff cooed.

Desdemona and Carley-Rue both glared at her.

"Besides you, I mean!" she said. "You're obviously the most beautiful child in the Cove, Carley-Rue!"

"The Problim girl doesn't even have a crown," Carley snarked.

"You know, they are just children," Dorothy said. "There's nothing to be afraid—"

Bertha jumped into the golf cart beside Dorothy and screamed, "Drive away. Now! Go! HIT THE GAS, DOROTHY LOU!"

"Why?" Desdemona asked as the sisters sped away into the fog. "Where are you going?"

Noah Wong's eyes shined with surprise. And then joy. Even as he sped his sister away from there, he couldn't help but look back. Magic. That's the only word he could think of—maybe the Problims really were capable of magic.

Because hundreds of spiders with shiny blue legs were scrambling down the cobblestone sidewalks. The clicking noise of their feet made it sound like they were tap dancing. Despite the screaming and running, the spiders never veered for the MOOS. They clickity-crawled in perfect unison . . . and disappeared through the foggy gate of House Number Seven.

"I'm starting the petition immediately!" Desdemona yelled.

Welcome Gifts

"Your fog garden is freaking out the neighbors," Mona told Sal as she pushed her scooter through the gate. "It's wonderful to see." Fuzzy, blue-legged spiders came scampering through the gate behind her and crawled up into the trees.

"Good," Sal said. He sat on the ground pulling the weeds that circled a yellow rosebush, with Ichabod beside him. "I'm sick of the neighbors looking through the gate. And for your information, if you hadn't tried to blow up my old garden, we could have stayed where we were. With *no* neighbors to worry about."

"Things happen." Mona kneeled down beside

him. "And anyway, I did some thinking on my morning promenade. I think Wendell and Thea are right. I think we should get to know the neighbors better." She smiled menacingly.

Sal shook his head. "The circus spiders will help us figure out why they're so afraid of us."

"Circus spiders are too slow. Let's go play with the neighbors."

"Sundae doesn't like the way you play with people."

"Sundae isn't here."

"She is, actually," Sal confirmed. "She's building tiny, portable homes for the homeless in the backyard."

The kitchen door opened, and Wendell and Thea scampered outside.

"Our sp-spiders!" Wendell shouted. "They're home!"

Thea kneeled and cupped a spider in her hand. She tapped its fuzzy head and smiled. "We're so sorry about the explosion, friend."

The twins had spent weeks training the spiders to do new tricks: acrobatics, one-legged web walking, fifteen-spider pileups—it would have been a spectacular show!

"Maybe we'll plan another spider circus some-day," Thea said. "When we're friends with the neighbors, they can come watch."

"B-brilliant!" Wendell agreed. His polka-dot bow tie matched Thea's cardigan. When they were little, the twins had liked dressing matchy-matchy. These days, Thea had a harder time convincing Wendell it was a good idea.

"Good morning, M-Mona!" Wendell smiled. "How's Fiona?"

Mona looked down at her darling flytrap. "The flies here aren't juicy enough. We miss the swamp."

"I d-don't!" Wendell said, spinning around. "Look at this garden! It's spect-tacular! I knew it would be. As soon as I saw this place, I thought: I cannot w-wait for Saturday!" On Saturday, Sal's day, the world bloomed. It bloomed in the rain or through the snow.

Sal's fog created a lovely dome over the plants. Underneath that dome, Sal had transformed the scraggly grounds of the Problim mansion into a fine garden almost overnight. Only a few days on Main Street, and thorny rosebushes were prickled with color. Mugwort and thistle mingled with ivy and cat-nip. Smelly herbs grew in the middle of the garden.

Moss dangled from the trees, blowing ghostly in the morning breeze, making the whole place look creepy-beautiful. Which was the best kind of beautiful, as far as the Problim children were concerned.

"What's this contraption thing?" Thea asked. Then she froze. "Wait . . . did you build this or did Mona?"

"Don't worry." Sal smiled. "Wendell helped me build it. And it's the reason for the fog. Behold my recycling-hydroponic garden. With a bit of humidity, it makes its own water *and* fog."

"Amazing," Thea said. Wendell had always loved water the way Sal loved land. Back in the swamp, Wendell had been the best swimmer. He could outswim an alligator; she'd seen it. "Twins for the win."

Thump, *bump.*

Sal nodded. "And thanks to the fog, the neighbors aren't peeking their nosy heads in the gate to spy on us."

Thea glanced at Wendell. He nodded at her. "Wendell and I think it's time to meet the neighbors."

"So I made c-cookies," Wendell said. He proudly opened the box to reveal skull-shaped chocolate chip cookies, with red-icing hearts for eyes.

Thea smiled. "Won't the neighbors love them?" She returned her attention to Sal. "Midge Lodestar, my life coach, says you can overcome your fear of meeting people by offering them gifts. And maybe if they liked us—if we were their friends—they wouldn't make us leave. I mean . . . we haven't found Problim proof, right?" She added quietly, "And Sundae still hasn't heard back from Mom and Dad."

Sal shook his head. "Midge Lodestar gives terrible advice. And besides—have you noticed they're not giving *you* gifts? They don't like us. They want to be left alone."

"Everybody needs friends! At first, we thought we'd give them circus spiders . . . ," Thea reasoned. (Mona's eyes glistened at this idea, but none of her siblings noticed.) "But the spiders have a job to do. So we made cookies instead."

"Which neighbors are you going to see? We have loads." Mona opened the cookie box and nodded at Wendell's creations. "I'd like to play with them all. . . ."

"L-Loads?" Wendell asked. "We'll need more cookies."

"Don't worry." Mona smiled, taking the box from her brother. "I'll go get the rest."

Sal rolled his eyes and returned to trimming the hedges that were trying to suffocate a lovely little bonsai tree. "I can't stop you from going out to meet the weirdos, but take my advice: Cove people are superstitious nuts."

Thea narrowed her eyes. "Sal . . . do you know something you aren't telling us?"

"I know tons of things that I never tell anybody." He laid his shears down. He reached to snap a thorny vine from the ground. "Just don't be surprised if the neighbors don't like you."

Sal's advice felt like a punch in the heart to Thea. Why would people hate someone they didn't even know?

Wendell patted her shoulder. "It's o-okay. We can at least try."

"Thea-Wendell! Here you go!" Mona said, running into the garden again. She smiled sweetly as she passed the cookies. "Have fun."

"Want to c-come along, Mona?"

"I considered it." Mona glanced up at the old Victorian behind her. Brimming with opportunities. Hiding places. Secrets. She smiled. "But I'm going to explore the house. Alone."

Introductions

Mrs. Wong flung open her front door at the sound of the buzzer. She was terrified. And elated.

Terrified because three of the demon children were on the doorstep, holding a box that contained God-knows-what. A dead bird? A beating heart? There were all sorts of rumors!

Elated because she couldn't wait to tell the rest of the girls in MOOS that the Problim children had actually come to her house. She never had anything exciting to share. Now excitement rested on her doorstep.

"Hello there," Thea said, lifting the box. "I'm Thea Problim!"

Wendell opened his mouth to say hello, but Thea talked for him. "These are my brothers Wendell and Toot."

Toot nodded once, gentlemanly. He'd picked a pink bow tie for the visits.

A boy Thea's age came running up behind his mom and shouted, "Is it true about the spiders?"

Mrs. Wong cupped her hand around her son's mouth. "What do you need?"

Wendell couldn't make eye contact with Mrs. Wong anymore. He was too excited to be in close proximity to another living, breathing human child that wasn't related to him. Wendell opened his mouth to speak, but Thea beat him to it.

"I'm Thea! This is my twin, Wendell. It's nice to meet you!"

"I'm Noah," he mumbled. But Thea was good with mumbles. Noah's mom kept her hand on his shoulder so she could pull him back in case the Problim children attacked.

"We live in the funny old house over there, the one with the pretty fog all around it."

"Wicked awesome!" Noah shouted.

"And we brought you gourmet cookies!" Thea said.

Mrs. Wong clutched the doorframe. "We don't eat cookies."

Thea nodded reassuringly. "You might eat these! They're gluten-free and peanut-free. Our big sister is allergic to both. Wendell made sure no peanuts were harmed in the making of these treats!"

Noah's eyes were sparkling. But his mother remained firm in her decision.

"Absolutely. No. Cookies!"

Noah yanked his mom's hand away from his mouth long enough to shout, "I LOVE COOKIES!"

Mrs. Wong shoved Noah inside and stomped out onto the stoop, slamming the door behind her. "No, thank you. You should go."

Wendell opened the box to show her the gooey, delicious skull-shaped cookies inside. Mrs. Wong's face froze in a picture of perfect fear. Her jaw twitched. She lifted a shaking hand to her mouth, as if she was trying to contain vomitus spew.

Thea felt her brother stiffen beside her. He started to speak to Mrs. Wong, when Thea became instantly defensive. "Listen here, lady! My brother is a baking wizard. If you don't like delicious desserts, well, that's a sad way to live. But it's your choice. There's no need to be so dramatic."

Mrs. Wong answered with a scream. Her shriek was so loud that Toot covered his ears and farted a 217.[13] The slamming door blew Thea's hair into her face.

"Oh, boo." Thea sighed. "Wendell, look. Mona put some circus spiders in here."

Wendell rolled his eyes and helped Thea lift the spiders gently from the box. She deposited one in each front pocket of her polka-dot cardigan. Usually the spiders preferred to travel on Thea's shoelaces, but they'd just been screamed at. So she wanted them close to her heart, where they would feel cozy and loved.

"We'll have to go b-back home for another b-box," Wendell said.

But they returned to find that Mona had reached those first as well. The icing smelled mysteriously of habanero peppers and toothpaste, so the gourmet desserts had to be chucked. Since the cookies had been sabotaged, Thea decided to take some of Sal's roses to the next house. One rosebush was full of fluffy yellow blooms. A perfect way to suggest

---

13 **#217**: The Shockfart: A flatulation of sudden elation, shock, or surprise. Smells like wet dog food mixed with applesauce.

a blossoming friendship!

"Something s-stinks," Wendell said as they waited at the next door. He and Thea both looked down at their baby brother.

Toot shook his head.

"I don't think he's let one rip for a while now," Thea reasoned.

The door flung open. A girl about their age wearing a soccer T-shirt and ballet tutu jumped out on the front step. She had brown skin and bright brown eyes and half of her head was shaved. She looked super cool, and a little bit strange, and Thea wanted to be her friend instantly.

"Don't talk," the girl said quietly, glancing over her shoulder. "I have three things to say to you. Thing one: my name's DeLisa, but everybody calls me LeeLee. Thing two: that fog thing you guys are doing? Amazing. Thing three: my mom thinks you might not be safe to play with. She doesn't want to sign that stupid petition, but she said we shouldn't hang out till she meets your parents—"

"What petition?" Thea asked.

"Shh!" LeeLee said. "Keep your voice down. The petition Ms. O'Pinion started to get you sent off somewhere. Anyway, if Mom sees you out here she'll . . ."

LeeLee's nose wrinkled. "Gawd. What's that smell?"

Toot waved.

"Number 124," Thea said happily. "That's his excited fart!"

LeeLee smiled at the baby. "He has different kinds of farts? That's awesome. That's cooler than a mood ring."

"LeeLee?" her mom hollered from inside. "Who's at the door, babe?" LeeLee's face dropped in sadness as her mom stepped out on the porch.

LeeLee mouthed, "You should probably gooo . . ."

Thea summoned her courage and said: "I'm Thea, and this is my twin, Wendell, and our little brother, Toot. We brought you a gift!" Thea pushed the flowers up into the fearful face of LeeLee's surprised mom. "We're your new neighbors, and we—"

The woman gagged and pulled LeeLee back inside.

"We're sorry! We didn't mean to—" Thea tried, but the door was shut firmly in her face.

"This is hopeless." Thea sighed.

Wendell shrugged. "Most things in life are hopeless. By the w-way . . . why do you always introduce me?"

"What?"

"I was just th-thinking about it. You say I'm your twin and then you keep going. I don't even t-talk."

"Well, you are my twin. And you don't like to talk!"

"It's not that I don't l-like to. I mean, it takes a while to s-say what I want. But maybe they won't care." He shrugged. "I could t-try."

"Oh. Of course you can. I didn't mean to make you upset or anything. I just thought I was helping," she told him. She lifted Toot up into her arms and tromped down the steps.

"It's just that I'm m-more than just your twin," Wendell said softly.

Thea spun to stare at her brother. He hadn't said those words in an angry way. But they still stung when they hit her heart.

"What's wrong with being my twin?"

"N-nothing." Wendell looked at the ground. "I guess I just w-want to be me too. If that makes sense. I think everybody forgets that we're two different p-people. Sometimes I think I f-forget."

And this time her heart went thump . . . and there was no bump behind it.

Everything was changing.

Of course she knew they were two different people, but she liked knowing he was always there with her too. She needed him there. Without Wendell, she'd never feel brave. Never want to leave the house, even. And what was so wrong with being her twin? It had never been a big deal before.

Toot tapped Thea's chest, just above her heart. He reached for his big brother and did the same, tapping above his heart until they were all three connected.

Toot popped a soft #78.[14] His chin wobbled.

"No worries, Toot." Thea assured the baby. "We're good."

But for a time, none of them spoke—not with their words, not with their hearts.

And then Wendell wrinkled his nose and lifted Sal's flowers for a sniff.

"Ugh!" he said, stepping backward. "Sal's engineered them to smell like a fart garden."

Thea sighed. "We're doomed when it comes to friends."

"We're doomed anyway." Wendell shrugged.

---

14 #78: The Peace Keeper: A toot reminiscent of steamy cow poo in a sunlit field. Meant to be calming but is actually rancid.

"I don't know what's more scary—no word from Mom and Dad or that awful petition. Why does Ms. O'Pinion hate us so much?"

"I don't know if she h-hates us or if she just wants our house."

"But she has a house already! It doesn't make sense."

Toot tugged on Wendell's sleeve as they walked down the street. He pointed to the tower room of the house next door. Number Five. The O'Pinion house.

Thea shook her head. "We are NOT going there."

Toot stopped walking and scrunched up his face. Thea didn't know if her baby brother was concentrating or trying to pick the perfect fart to communicate his feelings. He lifted his chubby arms above his head, curving his hands until his fingers were almost touching, like a ballerina.

"Astronaut?" Wendell asked.

Toot beamed as Wendell swung him up into his arms.

"I don't think we have any astronauts next door," Wendell assured him. "They're all in the sky, floating around drinking s-stardust milkshakes."

But Toot shook his head affirmatively and pointed again.

Thea looked to the tower room of the O'Pinion house . . . but only saw a fluttering curtain in the window. As though someone had been standing there watching and silently moved away.

A creeping-familiar feeling of excitement prickled against Thea's heart.

Maybe their house wasn't the only one with secrets.

⸜⸝

Later that night, the O'Pinions sat around their long dining table. Desdemona hummed happily as she typed an email to her friends at the Society for the Protection of Unwanted Children.

Orphans!

> Degenerates!

>> Unwanted!

>>> Unsupervised!

>>>> The entire neighborhood
>>>> is terrified!

She couldn't stop smiling.

Will was absorbed in his CosmicMorpho world. Carley-Rue pushed the fettuccini on her plate around with her fork, shaping it into a cheesy crown. And Joffkins hammered out an endless line of emails on his computer.

Carley-Rue sighed. "Has anyone seen Miss Florida 1987? She didn't come for dinner today. I'm worried about her."

"Weird." Will pushed up his mask. "Noah Wong said his family lost their cat too."

Tears wet Carley-Rue's eyelashes. Desdemona froze. "Has to be the Problim children."

Stealing cats! she typed quickly.

A small, shadowy silhouette filled the wall across from the doorway leading to the tower room. The shadow looked like a normal, tiny human body from the neck down. And a bubble from the neck up. "Hey there, fam! Just . . . letting you know I'm on my way down!" a little girl declared; her voice sweet but full of static, as though being spoken through a speaker.

"No! Wait!" Joffkins raced to the foot of the stairs. "What's wrong, sweetheart? Why do you need to come down?"

There was the sound of a throat clearing and then a girl's soft but strong voice. "I don't *need* to. But I am going to come down. I've decided that I'm having dinner with you tonight."

"No, no, sweetheart." Joffkins ascended the stairs, until the shadow was eclipsed by his own. "You can't."

"I'm wearing my mask, Dad! It's fine!"

"I said *no*." That was the final declaration her father made. "I'm sorry. But we have new neighbors."

"So?" the girl asked.

"They are rotten and dirty," Desdemona yelled. "And they smell like flatulence!"

"They must have been living under a bridge," Joffkins added. "Or in a dump, maybe. Because they were covered in ash and dirt and now the air quality outside is horrible. You might get sick if you come down tonight. Go back in your room. Quickly." He turned her gently, pushing her back toward the tower room he'd had designed and painted and decorated just for her. So she would love it. So she would always feel like a princess overlooking the kingdom, even if she couldn't be out in it. So she would never want to leave it.

"Hmph," Desdemona grumbled as she pushed away from the table to spy at the window. Again. Joffkins rubbed his tired eyes as he came to stand beside her.

Desdemona tapped her long red fingernail against the glass. "Do you see that? That shadow slinking through their yard? It's the boy one."

"The one that smells like farts?"

"No, the one with blades on his sleeves. I should call the police! He's probably scheming."

Carley-Rue raced to the window. "He's taking out the trash, Mom."

Desdemona nodded. "There's probably a body in the bag."

"It's trash!" Carley-Rue rolled her eyes. "It's a free country. He can walk around in his own yard."

"It's not *his* yard," Desdemona reminded her. "He's plotting. He's trouble." They'd all looked like trouble to Desdemona. Except the girl on the scooter. She was pretty, though. Too pretty. She could ruin Carley-Rue's chances of being next year's Corn Dog Princess for the fourth year in a row.

Joffkins sighed. "Desdemona—"

"The Problim family is dangerous! Terrible things happen when they're in town. The river dries up. The rain goes away. They'll probably evaporate the ocean somehow! You know why nobody's gone looking for those kids out in the Swampy Woods? Because the weather in the woods is wild and crazy and . . . bewitched, probably! Plus, they made *him* crazy."

Joffkins held up his hands. "Desdemona, I'm tired

of talking about them. Listen, I'm leaving tomorrow for several days, for the medical conference in Hoboken. Please keep an eye on Violet."

Desdemona shrugged. "She rarely comes out of her tower. The maid leaves her dinner at the door. I doubt I'll see her."

"She's been persistent lately. Sometimes I worry she'll try going out. Even if I say no."

Desdemona waved the notion away. "She'd never do that. You're lucky, Joff. Your daughter loves you, and she'd never disobey you."

Jaunty violin music drifted from the downstairs rooms. Music happened every night in the O'Pinion house. But the music was usually melancholy. Tonight the sound was almost . . . jubilant, dancing in time to the flickering candles. This was the kind of music that brightened the corners of your heart. Made you wonder. And remember. And think far, far too much. Desdemona hated it. But she wouldn't dare tell the musician not to play.

Joffkins looked toward the music, and then to his sister. "We live like ghosts in this house, all of us. Does that seem strange to you?"

"We live peacefully," Desdemona says. "That's

what a home should be. A perfect place of peace."

The music came to a crescendo, as if the person playing were overjoyed. A rising song, like birds soaring.

Joffkins tilted his head. "Do you think he knows about those children? That they're here?"

"Oh yes," Desdemona said, scraping her fingernail down the window so it made the faintest scream. "There's nothing that he doesn't know."

A Catapult
(and a Witch . . . Maybe)

Most squirrels don't notice spiders, but the purple-tailed squirrel was different. It was old enough to know circus spiders were the most special of all web spinners. First, because they could be trained to do tricks.

Second, because their webs caught rumors, not bugs.

So the squirrel settled into the nook of the old oak tree in the garden of House Number Seven, swishing his purple tail back and forth. Watching the spiders weave.

Usually circus spiders needed time to acclimate to

their new home before they tried any new endeavor, be it trapeze swinging or catching rumors. But circus spiders had always loved, and gravitated toward, the wild children in the swamp. It was as if being near them again made them feel at home. Already, thick, sparkling webs stretched across the tree branches. And every so often a bubble got caught there.

That's what rumors look like when they sail through the air: shiny, trembly soap bubbles. Rumors play out inside the bubbles, like tiny movies.

The squirrel twitched its mechanical whisker and peered closely at the collection of rumor bubbles trembling on the lines:

White-haired Frank Problim running down Main Street with something hidden under his coat.

Someone reading a newspaper story about the feud. TOO FAR THIS TIME? the headline read. TOWN SIDES WITH STAN O'PINION!

Seven children with dirty faces standing around a cauldron, chanting.

A girl with a long braid, her hand lifted to the river, sending the water up into the sky.

Another headline: DID BEWITCHED CHILDREN MAKE THE TOWN GO DRY?

And another: SPIDER INFESTATION! FOLKS BLAME THE PROBLIM CHILDREN.

The O'Pinion house as it was being built—with parts added, portholes carved into walls, and telescopes fitted on every porch corner.

And then . . .

The squirrel leaped to a higher branch and tilted its head sharply.

Inside this bubble was an image of one shadowy figure of a man . . . holding another from the edge of a plank—the same plank extending from the O'Pinion house.

Thieves! a bubble proclaimed. *Dark magic! Bewitched siblings . . . attempted murder?*

These were the rumors presently flying through the neighborhood.

They were only rumors, of course. But the squirrel

knew that there was a pinch of truth in some of those tales. This was no ordinary band of seven siblings.

Squirrels know true magic when they see it.

From the rumor webs, Thea and Wendell figured the town believed their grandfather had been a thief. A magical thief. With magical siblings. And he tried to throw someone off a roof. Or something.

(Reading a rumor web is difficult, after all. Rumors burst so easily.) Regardless, Thea and Wendell still believed they should convince the neighbors they were nice, fun to play with, and generally awesome. They assumed that would be difficult, considering parents wouldn't let their children anywhere near the Problems. But they were wrong.

"They're w-watching us," Wendell whispered as he adjusted his paper chef's hat. It was a typical afternoon: the twins were cooking outside, Sundae was off adventuring, and Frida was strumming her ukulele from the trees, a dirty foot dangling. Toot played with Ichabod. And Mona and Sal were creating.

THOMP!!!

Mona launched another squash from the human catapult she and Sal had spent the morning building.

"Who is watching?" Thea asked her twin. He pointed to the gate, where the neighborhood children stood, peering through the fog.

"Yay!" Thea shouted as Mona's squash splattered on the ground in front of her. "Come in, friends!"

LeeLee clutched the bars of the gate. "I'm doing it. I'm climbing over."

"Not yet, LeeLee!" Noah grabbed her shirt and pulled her back. "Mom says they're dangerous."

LeeLee nodded. "I like danger."

"C-come on in!" Wendell said. "We're having a smoothie smash! It's the most fun you'll ever have b-barfing."

LeeLee froze midclimb. "There's nothing fun about barfing."

Thea explained that the point of the game was to mix together all the ingredients you could find into a smoothie. And then see who could take a drink without throwing up. At first, there were no volunteers. In fact, the children stared blankly at Wendell and Thea.

THOMP!!!!

A small pumpkin sailed through the atmosphere.

Mona cleared her throat. "Anybody want to ride on the human catapult?"

"We have helmets and parachutes!" Sal added.

"I do," Noah Wong whispered. "I was born for this."

He climbed the gate, and LeeLee scrambled up beside him. "Me too! Look out, sky! Here comes LeeLee!"

Thea raced to help LeeLee and Noah over while Wendell opened the gate for the others. New friends! *Finally!* But the fun never begun, because of the MOOS stampeding down the street, screaming for their children.

"Noah!" His mother came running. "Noah! Get away from them!"

The other MOOS soon followed. They hurriedly pulled their children away from the Problims.

Mrs. Wong's nostrils flared. "First you covered the neighborhood in fog. Now you're playing these dangerous games. You were going to launch my son!"

"We always provide parachutes if we launch people," Sal assured her. "And by dangerous games, do you mean trimming the rosebushes? Or baking cookies? Or taking the pig for a walk?"

Mrs. Wong shook her head. "I mean, neighbor-hood cats just happened to disappear after you

showed up. And Desdemona O'Pinion strongly hinted that you were to blame."

Sal raised his eyebrows. "For disappearing cats?"

"I saw your sister petting one a few days ago. And talking to it."

"Mona was petting a cat?"

"No, the other sister."

"So Frida was petting a cat?"

"Frida? Who's Frida? No, the short, smiley blond girl was petting the cat! I think she stole it."

Sal stepped toward Mrs. Wong. His blades made a swishing sound under his jacket. "Sundae loves animals. She wouldn't steal one unless it was being mistreated."

Mrs. Wong pulled Noah close, though he didn't really want to be pulled. Like the other children, he was entranced by the Problims, and he wanted to find out more about them. He didn't mind the neighborhood fog. It made the street look like Halloween twenty-four seven.

Mrs. Davenport spoke next. "You should know, we've signed the petition. We've written a directive to the Society for the Protection of Unwanted Children to find new homes. For all of you."

113

Thea's heart felt like a hollow place. "You'd try to get rid of us?"

"Not only get rid of you," Mrs. Timberwhiff assured them. "But split you up. It's obvious you're even more vicious when you're together."

Thea didn't know what to say. The Problim family had never, ever considered that they might lose one another. All along, she'd thought the sevens were piling up because her parents were in danger. But maybe her siblings were in danger too. Separation was the worst danger of all.

Noah Wong looked up at his mom. "Okay, things got out of hand, and I'm sorry. But the Problims aren't bad—"

"Shh."

The entire crowd stilled. A low, creaking sound was coming closer from somewhere down the foggy street. At first, the sound reminded Thea of the robosquirrel's legs squeaking whenever it moved. But this was no squirrel.

This time, the sound came from the old, squeaky wheels of a baby carriage, and the silhouette of a tall person pushing that carriage down the sidewalk in the mist. Gradually, Thea could see more of the contraption: it was old and leathery-black. The umbrella roof was raised even though there was no sun that needed shielding. The woman pushing the carriage was tall, with lovely posture, but she was older than anyone else Thea had seen on Main Street. Long white hair feathered from underneath her straw hat as a cool breeze blew across the park. If a winter storm could take the form of a person, it'd be her, Thea thought.

"It's the widow," Noah whispered.

"Don't look at her," Mrs. Timberwhiff spoke softly. Thea heard a tremble in Mrs. Timberwhiff's voice, as if she were afraid of the woman. The MOOS all gathered their children and began to speak in low whispers to one another. Those whispers got caught in the spider webs, bulging and bulbous and full of lies. One bubble caught Thea's eye: *a witch on a broomstick*.

"A witch?" Thea said.

"SHHH!" all the MOOS and their children shushed her at the same time.

Still, the Problim children did not look away from the old woman. She didn't seem that scary to them.

The widow slowly pushed her carriage past the gate with her head held high. She had a strong jaw-line, and though her straw hat covered her eyes,

Thea believed they were probably noble. Thea was right. As the widow passed by, she looked over and smirked at the women who wouldn't look at her. Then she looked at Thea.

And Thea did the first thing that came to mind: she smiled.

The woman did not smile back, but her cheeks trembled like she might.

"People say she's crazy," Noah whispered softly. "She lives in a cottage on the edge of the woods— like the witch in *Hansel and Gretel*. My mom says its best to never make eye contact with her. And never go walking alone in Bagshaw Forest."

It wasn't crazy that Thea had seen in the widow's eyes. It looked more like loneliness, maybe. The woman pushed the carriage on down the street, until she was finally eclipsed by the fog.

"Who is she really?" Thea asked the crowd of cackling MOOS.

Mrs. Timberwhiff snorted. "She might be the only problem worse than a Problim. The Widow Dorrie, she's called. She lives in a cottage down the path on the far end of Main Street—just at the boundary of Bagshaw Forest. Her home doesn't fit the style of our new town—it's as bad as House

Number Seven—but we can't convince her to move. Enough of this! Time to go home."

The Problims stood in their yard, watching as the guests disappeared down the street.

"We're d-doomed," Wendell said.

Thump, *bump*. *Agree*, Thea heartspoke. "Maybe we should go hide in the Swampy Woods."

"But the wattabats bite this time of year!"

"Actually," Sal clarified, "they just think we're not good enough to live on their street."

"They don't think that lady is either," Thea told him as they took off down the street. "I don't understand these people."

Frida agreed:

"Maybe what makes a witch, in a town so
     small,
Is that she has no friends at all."

A Memory (and a Visit)

Later that night, Thea lay on a blanket in the Room of Constellations with Ichabod cuddled beside her. She looked at the painted stars, and she thought about her mom.

On the night of each Problim birth, under a sky full of stars, their mama would coo the words of an old nursery rhyme:

Monday's child is fair of face,
Tuesday's child is full of grace,
Wednesday's child is full of woe,
Thursday's child has far to go,
Friday's child is loving and giving,

Saturday's child works hard for a living,
But the child who's born on the Sabbath day
  is good and wise in every way.

Many people knew that rhyme, but Mama added her own part to the end, which Thea found especially lovely:

Adventure waits—for good—forever—
to a perfect seven who work together.
But if seven bicker, and seven fall . . .
you can't have one without them all.
And so it goes, the treasure's spurned,
until the seven do return.

Mama Problim had told the rhyme like a story—when she tucked them into bed at night, when she led them on adventures through the Swampy Woods. Sometimes she even sang the rhyme to them.

Together, Thea thought. That was her favorite place to be. She thought of the sun setting in the Swampy Woods. She thought about swinging grapevines over the pond and eating wild blackberries and catching wattabats in mason jars. Watching their wings flicker, sparkle, shine.

She thought of her dad, teaching her how to train circus spiders. And showing her how to brush the dust off the fossil of a leaf.

She thought and she wondered and she hoped and she dreamed. And she worried. Always worried. She tried not to close her eyes, because as soon as she did, the nightmares would come back. Dreams about being forgotten, abandoned, all alone in the dark.

And so, to calm herself, Thea imagined telling her mom about the new neighbors.

And about Wendell being so weird lately.

And about the Widow Dorrie she'd seen earlier.

Her mom always helped her see the world in a new way: through telescopes and magnifying glasses. And also, of utmost importance, her mom would remind her to look at people in different ways too. "Look at someone heart-first," Mama Problim always said. "There's never an excuse to be cruel. When you meet someone new, think first about all the good and the sad and the wonder and the worry that's probably blooming in their heart. Just like yours."

Thinking about her mom gave Thea an idea.

She jumped out of the sleeping bag and raced

down the secret passage to the library. She was going to ask Wendell to go with her, but he'd fallen asleep in a chair reading a book. She hated going out into the darkness alone. But she knew Wendell would only be grouchy if she woke him up. She decided to take Ichabod instead.

Thea grabbed Sundae's flashlight from the kitchen and walked out the back door whispering Midge Lodestar's mantra:

"Every day is a good day for a taco!"

She found the path at the end of Main Street, but she couldn't see the widow's house. Fog billowed too thickly in the woods. Thankfully, there was a small mailbox at the edge of the path with the word "Leave" painted on the side. She put a note inside the box, with "Ms. Dorrie" written in bold letters.

Dear Ms. Dorrie,
I do not think you are weird. But if you are, I think that's snazzy. Please come by House Number Seven sometime if you'd like to be my friend, or have a cookie, or build an obstacle course. I am leaving

121

a flower too. Sorry if it smells like a happy fart. If you have a brother, I'm sure you'll understand.

Your friend,
Thea Problim

As Thea and Ichabod walked back toward the house, Thea was startled by a familiar swoosh of purple.

The squirrel was settled in the magnolia tree, face lifted toward the stars. And then it looked right at her. Something sparkled and whirred around its robotic eye. The music played again.

Was the squirrel a music box? Had it swallowed a music box?

And that melody . . . how did it know that melody . . .

Tell me a tale worth telling back . . .

Thea knew she was so close . . . to finding the lyrics . . . to remembering something important. She reached in the pocket of her hoodie and felt the smooth bone-stick she and her siblings had unearthed in the swamp. Was it all connected? It had to be, didn't it?

"What are you trying to tell me?" Thea asked.

Her voice felt so small when she was all alone, there in the darkness.

Once again, the squirrel seemed to wink its shiny eye. With the flick of its tail, it became a flash of silver, scampering away into the night.

The Princess Astronaut
Leaves the Tower

By the time most people on Main Street woke up the next day, the fog was thick, soupy; the same as it had been since the Problim children arrived. But long before they woke up—before the sun lightened up the ever-gray skies above the Cove—the fog around the Problim mansion bloomed.

And today it bloomed quite beautifully.

Shapes emerged from the fog: roses unfurling, horses galloping, ships with puffy, billowing sails. There were smaller images in the fog, too, bunnies and squirrels and gauzy-winged butterflies. This had always happened when Wendell read books to Sal's plants. It was as if the fog all around the garden—sometimes even the clouds—wanted to act out every scene in the story. Sal loved to hear his brother read. He would have loved it even if Wendell stumbled over words the way he did in conversation. But that never happened when he was reading.

The quiet between the brothers had always been nice, and it had always allowed a special kind of space for wonder to bloom. Sal listened thoughtfully to Wendell that morning, watching as the fog galloped and sailed and soared all around them. (Thea preferred sleeping in most mornings. "The early bird gets the worm," Midge Lodestar said. "But who needs a worm? Sleep in and catch the bird!")

Eventually the morning sun melted the fog and the shapes, and Sal scrambled to cover his dragon snappers. He leaned down to pull a twig from the ground . . . and noticed a strange shadow stretched out beside him.

The shadow of a bubble-headed monster.

Or an astronaut, maybe.

The shadow appeared to have a human body on the lower half . . . but the top was perfectly round and reminded him of a gumball machine.

Sal whirled around to hear the frightened squeal of a small girl. She was wearing the bubble like a helmet. Her hair was short, just touching her chin. She wore purple glasses, which framed a large set of frightened eyes.

"Who are you?" Sal asked.

She looked him over, head to toe, and her eyes widened at the sharp tools attached to his sleeves. She turned and ran.

Which might have been effective if her run had been less of a jog. The girl wasn't fast.

Neither was Sal. Tools were handy, but they weighed him down. He saw the girl veer toward the gate.

"Wait! Don't run that way!" Sal yelled. "You'll step in the—"

The girl stretched her arms for the lock but was surprised when something snagged her ankle and yanked her to the ground. The Wrangling Ivy coiled around her knee and dragged her back into the garden, helmet bumping along on the ground.

Wendell jumped into action this time: landing on the vine so Sal could cut the girl free. "Sorry about that!" Sal laughed as he leaned down to help her sit up. "I set that trap for my sister Mona."

"You tried," came Mona's fluttery voice from the tree above.

Her brothers screamed. "When did you get back, Mona?" Sal shouted. "And where have you been?"

Mona shrugged and jumped down. "Searching the house alone, like I said." She tilted her head at the stranger. "Oh. Sal, did you catch Toot's astronaut?"

The bubble girl looked around nervously. Sal wasn't so sure she could even speak.

Mona propped her fists on her hips "Tell us your name," she said sweetly. "Or I'll feed you to my Venus flytrap."

"Don't w-worry about her," Wendell said, kneeling down across from the astronaut. "Are you okay?"

"Let me know if you want me to torture a confession out of her," Mona said as she climbed back up in the tree. "And let me know when she's gone. I have something important to show you."

The girl blinked at Wendell. *She looks kind*, Wendell thought. In fact, she actually looked like a much nicer version of Mona. She looked so smart, so science-like, in her bubble hat. She was so . . . unique!

"I'm Violet," her voice crackled through speakers at the base of the bubble. "Violet O'Pinion. I live next door. That's an awesome birthmark you have."

"Oh," Wendell touched the pale-purple mark on his face. "Thanks. It's called a p-port wine stain. And sometimes it's called a firemark."

"Firemark sounds much better!" Violet's voice crackled happily. "It's like something a hero would have. Heroes in books have a special scar or mark sometimes, have you noticed?"

"You like to r-read?"

"No. I looove to read."

Toot waddled up behind his siblings. He farted a curious #104. Wendell nodded. "We call that fart 'the Questioner.' Toot wants to know why you are an astronaut, Violet."

She giggled, and her breath fogged up her glass bubble for a second. "It's only a helmet. A safety barrier, actually. I'm allergic to air."

"To *air*?" Sal asked.

She nodded. "My room is a safe place; the air there is processed and detoxified. But my father invented this barrier to keep me safe when I'm out. Not that I ever get to go out. It does come in handy, though, in case I encounter a batch of unpurified air. Or if Wrangling Ivy pulls me halfway across the neighbor's yard."

Sal raised an eyebrow. "You've heard of Wrangling Ivy?"

Violet nodded excitedly. She reached to touch the vine, which coiled happily under her fingertips. "I love gardens. I love science, really. It's so full of magic, isn't it? I watched you plant your garden from my window. And I watched the fog shapes. I hope you don't mind that I came down; I just wanted to see what you were planting up close. It's all so wonderful!"

Sal blushed. Toot puffed a #124.[15]

"S-sorry about that," Wendell said. "He farts a lot when he's happy."

"My mask purifies air, so it actually smells great to me." Violet grinned. "Like lime and honeysuckle!"

Toot waddled over to Violet and wrapped his tiny arms around her in a welcoming hug.

"I'm sorry we haven't met yet," Wendell said. "Everybody's afraid of us. Or afraid of our family, I guess."

"I heard," Violet said sadly.

"I was h-hoping we'd make friends in time to

---

15 **#124:** The Joyful, Joyful: Simple flatulence of happiness. Smells like a week-old bouquet of daisies.

have a birthday party for my twin, Thea, and me. But our birthdays are next week, so it's not looking g-good."

Violet's eyes brightened. "I think that's a great way to break the ice! Everybody loves a birthday party!"

"Will you c-come if we have one?"

Violet shook her head. "I've never been to any party. I've only been to my own birthday party. If my cousins have a birthday, my cousin Will always saves me a piece of cake."

"Oh, everybody gets their own cake at a Pr-Problim party!"

"I wish I could be there," she said. "But I don't think my aunt will let me."

"Is your aunt the cranky lady with the fingernail claws and big sunglasses?" Sal asked.

Violet nodded. "Be careful around her. Not that you'd ever be around her on purpose. But she's always wanted this house. She's obsessed with it. I'm pretty good at eavesdropping. I think she believes there's a treasure hidden in there."

The children all turned to look at the Problim mansion at the same time. Old curtains were half-drooped over the attic windows, as if the house were half-asleep. Or half-staring. They'd searched the house high and low for Problim proof for over a week now. Surely they would have noticed a treasure. Or . . . would they?

What, exactly, did people believe Grandpa had stolen? What was Desdemona so desperate to find?

Sal scratched his head. "Why didn't she sneak in there and look over the past seven years then? She's had a long time."

"She tried," Violet said. "But something strange always happened when she nearly got inside. Aunt Desdemona might act like she's not afraid of Frank Problim—or any of you. But she is. And she had to wait until the seven-year law was up."

A long black car emerged from the fog at the end of the street. Violet stood and ran for the gate. "That's her! Please don't tell her you saw me. I'm not allowed outside."

"Not e-even with your helmet?" Wendell asked.

"Not for any reason," Violet said, jogging through the fog, sidestepping the ivy, and disappearing through the gate. Wendell watched to make sure she made it back to her mansion next door. She waved once from her lonely window. And smiled.

Desdemona's car rolled to a stop on the edge of the Problim property.

Waiting.

"We might as well go see what she wants," Sal said. He looked at his siblings.

Toot nodded and clutched his fists. He tooted a #45.[16] Sal hoisted him up on his hip.

"Fun," Mona cooed as she hopped down from the tree. "Someone to toy with."

Wendell nodded. "C'mon. Problims, pile up."

The back window reflected the determination in their faces as the four Problim children walked toward it. Then it rolled down, revealing Desdemona O'Pinion.

"Good morning, children," she said, with the sort of voice that gave them chills. Like the storms that whisper thunder before they roll over a city; a warning to go back inside.

"So," Desdemona tapped her fingers on the side of the vehicle. "Have your parents come home yet?"

Sal spoke. "Our parents are grand—"

"Yes, yes," Desdemona said, a smile creeping

---

16 **#45:** The Braveheart Fart: The toot used by Toot to summon his courage and drive fear into his enemies' hearts. Smells like moldy cheese and sweaty victory.

across her face. "I remember. And I'm sure this business about some Queen of Andorra is *truth*. Because you know what happens to children who lie, don't you?"

Toot nodded fiercely.

Desdemona leaned forward. "Good. So unless you are absolutely sure your parents will be home before your days are up, you might want to leave now. Before you get caught."

"We aren't leaving!" Sal puffed his chest. "This is our house."

"This house," Desdemona growled, "is mine."

"B-because you believe there's a treasure inside it," Wendell said, surprised by the power in his voice. Thea would have been doing the talking for him if she were there. But she wasn't. And he was fed up with this—with someone being so cruel.

"So you do know where it is," Desdemona said softly.

"There are w-wonderful treasures in there. But they're family t-treasures. Nothing worth enough to make you happy."

"The treasure he stole from my beloved father was worth everything. To me. To this town. It could have changed the world. It will change the world,

Problims. You moved into this town generations ago and wrecked it. You stole something precious, something a child could never understand. You are not welcome here. Leave soon together. Or I'll see to it that you leave apart. Don't forget: seven children, seven continents . . ."

And only two weeks left, Wendell realized. He had to warn Thea. And Sundae too. Sevens were everywhere. And if Desdemona O'Pinion was involved, something terrible was definitely afoot.

"We're d-doomed," Wendell said as the car rolled away.

"No we aren't," Mona assured them. "Look what I found in the basement."

When Mona reached into her pocket, her siblings jumped away from her. It was a habit; they assumed she'd have some sort of poisonous bug or toad ready to throw. But there was no frog this time. Mona uncurled her fingers to reveal another bone-stick—long, and white, and gold at the edges.

"Another twig," Sal said with a sigh. "Too bad a twig can't prove who we are."

Friends Happen

"You made a friend?" Thea stared at her twin in disbelief.

"Y-yes!" Wendell nodded. "She came crashing into the yard! Did you hear the other part of what I said, though? Ms. O-O'Pinion stopped by to scare us."

Thea nodded. "I heard."

They were in the kitchen, rounding up all the baking supplies Wendell needed for their double-twintastic birthday party. Rain from Sal's plants drizzled down the windows and made shadow tears on Wendell's face. But he definitely wasn't sad. Everything about Wendell seemed to be smiling then, especially his eyes. They were bright and shiny.

"Her name's V-Violet, and she thinks we should invite the neighborhood to our b-birthday party. She seems super smart and c-cool. She's going to try to come too, even though her aunt doesn't let her out of their house."

"Oh."

"That's it? I thought you'd be excited! That's what you wanted most of all! To make f-friends!"

A new feeling—definitely not excitement—stirred up somewhere deep in Thea's heart. Something like anger mixed with dizzy-sickness. Mixed with fear. Mixed with sadness.

Is that what jealousy felt like? How could she be jealous of Wendell? She loved her brother more than anyone in the world. But the fact that he'd met Violet and couldn't stop talking about Violet and couldn't wait to have an adventure with *Violet* . . . it hurt somewhere deep. Wendell had a new friend already. Thea didn't.

Wendell shut his recipe book. "Why are you a-angry?"

"I'm not."

"I feel what you f-feel, Thea. I think you're just mad that I didn't need your h-help."

Tears watered in Thea's eyes when she glanced at her brother. He looked away instantly. An uncomfortable silence stretched between them. Wendell tried to change the subject.

"I was thinking maybe we c-could make the stairs into a water slide. On the day of the p-party."

"Maybe you should ask Violet what she thinks," Thea said softly. And she left the room on the verge of tears.

Sundae on a Mission

Before the sun woke up the next day, two Problim children were already adventuring.

Thea sat on the library floor, tucking invitations into envelopes. Ichabod snored beside her. She heard the happy hum of her oldest sister coming down the stairs. Sundae had thirteen tiny backpacks draped over her arms.

"Where you going?" Thea asked.

Sundae startled when her sister spoke. Then she giggled. "Off to the town library first. Andorra has decided to have a technology-free summer, which is great for them but . . . hard for us. I've tried to call and email. I was going to research the nearest city and send a letter there—"

"You're worried," Thea said. "I can see it in your eyes, Sundae. What if Mom and Dad don't get in touch with us in time? What if—"

"All is peachy-swanky-fine!" Sundae assured her. "I have a plan that's foolproof. Toodles!"

Before Thea could ask anything else, Sundae skipped quietly away. Thea could have sworn she heard a soft meow as the door opened, then closed.

Later on, Thea tucked her invitations in the circus spider tree. (Circus spiders also provide excellent delivery services.) And every child on Main Street woke to find a letter propped in their window:

WENDELL AND THEA ARE TURNING 12!

So let's swing from the trees!
Let's do as we please!
Let's have a wild party out back!
Bring bullfrogs and bugs,
Come prepared to give hugs!*
Visit once and you'll want to come back!

Saturday Night–Sunday Morning. • Beginning at 7:07 p.m.
Cake Smash at Midnight! • The Problim Home • #7 Main Street

PS Come absolutely any time! Why wait for the party?
RSVP by tomorrow, please!

*Ask first, please.
Not everyone wants their personal space invaded.

A Riddle and a Squirrel

Rain pattered against the roof of the Problim mansion, dripping through some of the old shingles and tapping splatters against the marble floor. The cake smash wasn't scheduled to start until midnight—so that both children could celebrate. Thea thought that fact alone would mean nobody came . . . but surprisingly everyone on Main Street had RSVP'd.

The children party planned in the library.

Frida strummed a ukulele, her fox ears pulled up over her head.

Sal studied the two bone-sticks on the library

desk and compared them to tree branches in a science volume he'd found. Unfortunately, they didn't match any tree in the book. Thea curled into a corner chair and tried to sketch a picture of the purple-tailed squirrel.

Sundae consulted a list of ideas. "Is there anything else I've missed for the big day tomorrow?"

"I have an idea for a game." Mona grinned.

To which they all replied, "NO!"

Frida continued playing. Eventually, Thea realized she was strumming a familiar song. This time Thea sang it out loud.

"*Tell me a tale worth telling back,*" Thea chirped.

Whack!

Whack!

Whack!

The sound was sharp against the window, a perfect punctuation to Frida's strumming.

"What is that?" Sal asked, racing to the window.

But just as he got there, the glass shattered. The mechanical squirrel zoomed through the opening like a fluffy rocket. With arms outstretched, it dived for the ground, rolling into a ball as it hit the floor. It pounced up immediately, and shook the glass away from its tail.

"That's the squirrel!" Thea and Wendell shouted at the same time.

Toot laughed and waved at the creature. He puffed a #213.[17]

Sundae scratched her head. "Did I miss something?"

The seven siblings surrounded the squirrel on the floor, finally able to get a good look at it.

"Wendell and I saw it in the Swampy Woods," Thea said.

"It looks animatronic," Sal told them.

The squirrel shook its fluffy face, loosening the stained glass embedded there.

"Is it like a d-drone?" Wendell asked.

Sal shrugged. "Maybe a little. It's a cool invention. Frank Problim was known for his animatronics. It could be his!"

The squirrel shook its tail excitedly at the mention of Frank Problim.

And then the music filled the room; the soft tinkling melody the squirrel always carried inside it.

~~~~~~~~~~~

17 **#213**: The Welcome Fart: This toot begins with the subtle smell of pineapple but ends on a note of sauerkraut.

"Tell me a tale worth telling back," Frida sang along to the music.

"And I'll sing you a new song, clackity-clack."

Wendell sang the next verse:

"Because life is still worth living, dear,
When the day is long and the dark is near."

"Grandpa's song," Sundae breathed. She cleared her throat and sang:

"Be brave and wild, and live it well,
Make your life the best story you'll ever tell . . ."

As they all joined in, the squirrel stood fully upright, as if it might salute. It scampered toward Thea and jumped on her arm.

"Whoa!" Thea shouted, balancing herself so the squirrel wouldn't fall. That's when she noticed a very small door where the squirrel's heart should be. A small door . . . with a small opening . . . for a small key.

"Sal!"

He'd seen it too; Sal pulled Frank's necklace from around his neck and inserted the key carefully. It was a perfect fit. And as his siblings leaned in, Sal pulled out a tiny paper scroll.

The rest of the Problims crowded around him.

"What's it say?" Thea asked, leaning over his shoulder to read.

"The writing is too small," Mona complained.
"Shh," Sal said. "I can see it fine. It says:

Hello, children, gather near,
There is a story you should hear,
a tale of sevens, odd but true,
and all the things that they could do.

Where seven seek, a treasure waits.
More riches than their hearts can take.

Adventure waits—for good—forever—
for a perfect seven who work together.
But if seven bicker, and seven fall . . .
you can't have one without them all.
And so it goes, the treasure's spurned,
until the seven do return.

"That's the last part of our birthday rhyme!"
Thea said. Sal continued:

You've found the first,
but you're not through!
There's plenty of work still left to do.

Seven pieces you shall find,
And seven hearts will be aligned.

Mr. Biv will show the way,
Where widows watch is where he stays.
Nestled there inside the beast,
Is the first clue for which you seek.
De Léon was right to dream.
But no treasure is ever what it seems.
Two lie where all adventures start;
The place where Wendell leaves his heart.
Another's hidden in plain sight,
knock and look—you'll see I'm right!
A small one in a darkened nook
might require a second look.

The last is in the dreamer's sights,
But it's up to you to make this right.
The witch will help, but you must lead.
Together you have all you need.

They all sat silently for seven seconds, then they all talked at once, babbling about riddles and treasures and witches and Grandpa Problim and—

"Quiet!" Sal pleaded.

Toot puffed a #227.[18]

Sal studied the riddle again. "He's basically admitting he did take this town's treasure. So the feud wasn't totally unfounded, it sounds like."

"And the bone-sticks have to be part of the treasure," Sundae reminded them. "We found the first in the lunch box!"

Mona cleared her throat. "And the one I found was in the darkest corner of the basement. I looked right over it a few times. It was so damp and dark down there. Like a dungeon." She grinned. "I would like to live in a dungeon . . ."

"Focus!" Sal groaned in frustration. "Old sticks aren't a treasure!"

"Read it again!" Thea said. "He said that a treasure isn't what it seems. Maybe nobody else understood the sticks but him. So he took them for a reason. And maybe he hid them for a reason—so the wrong people won't find them. So the right people will. Isn't that so exciting?" Thea leaned in. "The bone-sticks lead to something. We just have to find it!"

---

18 **#227**: The Hushfart: Softer sounding than a referee's whistle, but still shrill. Smells like gym class. Means: be quiet!

"Or f-find a witch," Wendell added. They were all silent at this. "What d-does any of this have to do with a witch? Was he talking about the widow, maybe? Some of the n-neighborhood kids called her a witch."

Thea had wondered the same. She shrugged. "All I know is that we need to find the treasure. And then we can return it. And everything will be okay then, right? Because then they'll let us stay until Mom and Dad finally get here. We have a week to find this thing."

"S-seven days," Wendell said softly.

"So we're looking for more sticks?" Sal asked. "And then we figure out what a witch has to do with any of this?"

Sal tried to sound grumpy, but Thea could hear a faint note of hope in her big brother's voice. Plus, he was still holding that key in his hands, tight between his fingers, the same way you hold a penny before you wish on it, and toss it in a fountain.

"Let's keep planning the party," Sundae said. "I really think the neighbors will adore us once they meet us. But let's also keep our eyes open and ears up," she said, tugging Frida's fox ear. "Let's ponder these clues, Problims! Because there's clearly a reason Grandpa wanted us here."

Birthday Smash Cake

One of the most popular rumors about the Problim children was that they had no manners, due to their wild, backwoods upbringing. But if there's one thing even the most proper person knows, it's this: backwoods people throw awesome parties.

The neighborhood would have shown up for the party alone, but the fact that nobody had been inside Frank Problim's mansion in years made them even more eager for the twins' celebration.

"Our first birthday party in our new home!" Sundae chirped. "Wendell and Thea will have the most swamptastic celebration."

Wendell picked up one of the invitations the circus spiders had issued that morning. "Even the m-mayor is coming!"

"Of course he is! Let's get the house in spiffy shape!" Sundae's eyes were dancing with the joy she got from doling out tasks and organizing things. "Okay, Problems. Report! Let's hear what we're doing! Sal?"

"I'm covering the exterior decorations. I've spruced up the plants and the garden looks pretty darn awesome. I'm also going to get out the rappelling gear and put some googly-eye glasses and hats on the gargoyles that sit on either side of the Porch of Certain Death."

"Yes! And Sal," Sundae said. "I do appreciate the lovely way you engineer flowers. But maybe no fart blossoms for the party, okay?"

Sal shrugged. Toot turned to her quickly with sad, questioning eyes.

Sundae pulled the baby into her lap and kissed his cheek. "You are always welcome, silly. You're the ultimate fart blossom. So! Sal's got the flowers. Toot's taking care of ambiance. Frida?"

Frida stood tall in the chair and said:

"After everyone's had some fun outside,
Those stairs become a water slide!
We'll have ourselves a bubbly romp.
Just like the parties
back home in the swamp."

"I adore that idea!" Sundae grinned. "It might ruin the floors, but won't it be fun to remodel once it's all over? Wendell is taking care of food—smash cakes for everyone, right?"

"Of c-course!"

"And I have an idea for a game." Mona beamed. "It's called 'Chase the Neighbors with Flaming Torches!'"

"NO!" they all shouted.

Thea scooted in closer, clasping her hands together. "Do you have anything special I can do, Sundae?"

Sundae chewed her lip as she concentrated. "Why don't you just jump in wherever someone needs help? And have fun."

"Okay," Thea said with a sad sigh.

And Thea did . . . whatever they told her to do. Then she left the room unnoticed and snuck back upstairs to her dreaming room. The room of stars.

"My Thursday girl," her mom had always called her. "She has wild hair and a wilder heart."

But what good was a wild heart if you weren't good at anything? What good was a wild heart if you were always afraid?

Thump . . . Thea hoped Wendell would come check on her. Maybe think of a new game they could play. But Wendell never came; he was too busy making treats for the party.

What good is a wild heart if your twin brother— your best friend in the whole world—didn't want to hang out with you anymore?

⁓

Over the next few hours, the mansion transformed. Sal and Wendell climbed up the outside to put sunglasses and party hats on the gargoyles watching from the Porch of Certain Death. Thea helped Frida inside; she couldn't stand watching the boys do something so dangerous. Her heart was drowning in fear, and she tried to push that feeling toward Wendell—so he'd feel it too and climb down.

But Wendell climbed anyway. When did he stop caring what she thought?

Once the gargoyles were decorated, Wendell rappelled down and read aloud to Sal's garden. The fog ballooned into the shapes of hearts and stars and floating crowns. Using a bow and arrow, Mona sent streamers around the roof. Sundae climbed the trees in the backyard, distributing tiny party hats she'd made for the bluebirds.

Sundae and Mona had wrapped one of Sal's twiggy plants around the upstairs rails. They found tiny fairy lights in an old trunk and wove them through the branches. Sundae made paper lanterns and hung them from the front porch. And Thea dusted off Grandpa Problim's wonderful record collection. Frida slid into the room dancing. She grabbed Thea's hand and spun around until they were dizzy with laughter. They didn't realize how late it was until they heard the doorbell ding. And then make a loud zapping sound with someone yelling, "OUCH!"

Mona chuckled softly.

The animatronic squirrel had stayed close to the Problims since it had shown up in the library. As Sundae walked toward the door, she scooped up the squirrel and looked deep into his sparkly, mechanical eyes. "We definitely need to keep you safe somewhere."

Toot offered to take care of him. And he puffed a #47[19] to prove it.

"I can always depend on you, Tooty-kins," she said, passing the squirrel to her baby brother. Sundae patted his fancy tweed hat, which he'd worn to match the bow tie stuck to his onesie with Velcro. The squirrel snuggled its cold, metal face against Toot's chest. The baby giggled. Sundae sat them both on the purple sofa beside the record player. "Everything ready?" she asked.

They all nodded.

"I'll keep the grown-ups here in the parlor," Sundae said as she scampered toward the door. "I have a slideshow on creating cushioned habitats for elderly owls that I want to share ahead of the party. Then we'll have a cake smash, a sing-along, and a water slide relay!"

"The spider woman isn't coming, is she?" Sal said, pulling small scissors from his sleeve to trim his plant. "Ms. O'Pinion? I don't trust her."

Sundae shook her head. "I . . . didn't send her an invitation. I felt guilty about it, honestly. I think she's

---

19 **#47**: The Defensive-Offensive: A toot used by Toot that creates an invisible, yet rancid, cloud of protection around those he loves.

probably a terrible person, since she wants to split us up and send us to the far corners of the earth. But even villains deserve cake!"

Thea hugged her arms across her chest. Because her wild heart was beating a *watch-out, watch-out* kind of rhythm. She looked to Wendell; surely he felt the same way. But he wasn't responding. "Ms. O'Pinion will probably come anyway," Thea said. "You think she'll pass up a chance to get inside?"

Sundae nodded. "Good point, Thea! So everybody stay on the watch for her, okay? I don't want her rummaging through the house when we're not looking."

"Because we have seven days," Thea reminded them. "Have you heard from Mom and Dad yet, Sundae?"

"They'll be here," Sundae reassured them. And then she quickly changed the subject. "Wendell, bring out snacks whenever you want. Just remember to serve slowly, not all at the same time. And now, I shall bestow upon Wendell and Thea the Problim party hats!" Sundae placed old felt top hats on each of their heads. Thea's fit low on her forehead. "This is your party. Enjoy it!"

"I wish V-Violet could come," Wendell said.

And Thea felt another bee sting of jealousy in her heart. Some girl next door had enchanted her brother. And now he had a friend. And Thea didn't. And Wendell was probably imagining all the adventures he'd have with Violet instead of her.

Maybe this is how twelve feels, Thea thought. Maybe the world flip-flops, goes upside down. But not in a fun way. In a rotten way. Maybe everything changes, especially the things you want to stay the same.

"And!" Frida said with a spin:

*"We'll keep our eyes
open wide
for a treasure
beyond measure!"*

Thea shrugged. "We've looked everywhere, I think." The clues seemed so bogus. The place where Wendell leaves his heart; that was obviously the library. So they'd checked all the funny animatronics on the shelves, thinking they might have a secret door like the squirrel. But they didn't. *Nestled there inside the beast . . . in the dreamer's sights.* None of the clues made sense, really.

The fox flipped into a trembly handstand and said:

"Like a smile becomes a frown,
We should look upside down!"

Frida lost her balance and flopped into a statue of a flamingo, which hit the ground and shattered.

Someone banged on the door.

"I'm afraid," Thea admitted. "Letting people in our home . . . it's scary, isn't it? This is our space. This is the first time other people have been invited in. What if the kids are mean, like their parents? What if they take our things? What if . . ."

"What if they n-need us?" Wendell asked. "Everybody needs Problems."

"Everything will be all right," Sundae said. But her voice didn't sound as happy as usual. Even she was afraid. Because opening the door to your home is not so different than opening the door to your heart. What if you let someone in and they destroy something you love?

❧

"What an interesting toy for a little boy," said Mrs. Wong as she regarded Toot's mechanical squirrel.

Most of the kids were outside playing games, but Toot stayed in the parlor. He offered Mrs. Wong a deep-dimpled grin and farted a #173.[20] Mrs. Wong laughed; she adored babies and was completely smitten with Toot's stinky cuteness.

So far so good, thought Thea. With shaky hands, she refilled Mrs. Wong's tea. Then sniffed it subtly to make sure Mona hadn't deposited anything creepy into the teapot. "He loves animals! I think our grandmother loved animals too. I see all sorts of animal statues around here."

"Oh, I remember your grandma!" said Bertha. She elbowed Dorothy's arm. "Dorothy here knew your grandfolks better than me, even."

"It's true!" Dorothy beamed, kicking her tiny cowboy boots back and forth. She was so short her feet didn't touch the floor. "Your grandma, Penny, used to keep a whole miniature zoo there in the garden. Some animals were real. Some were animatronic. And like your sister over there," Dorothy gestured to Sundae's slideshow, "Penny had a soft place in her heart for animals. Especially animals

---

20 #173: The Appreciation Flatulation: A soft, graceful puff of wind that means: thank you. Smells like toe jam and strawberry jam mixed together.

who were a little bit broken and a little bit different. And like you, she was great at making folks feel welcome in a place."

Thea's heart seemed to bloom, fast and full like one of Sal's swamp flowers. Knowing she had something in common with her grandma made her heart feel so warm, so light. Suddenly she wanted a thousand more details. "Do you remember anything else about my grandma?"

"I know a few things!" Dorothy nodded eagerly. "Penny was an artist. Wore lots of strange dresses. Especially liked ones with bird prints on them— feathers and seagulls and hummingbirds. That's what your grandpa called her, you know. Hummingbird. He told people that's how he felt the first time he saw her. Like his heart was flat-out fluttering inside the cage of his chest."

"Really?" Thea sighed. The most wonderful picture filled up her imagination; her grandfather coming in from a long day at work and kissing her grandma's soft cheek. *Hello, Hummingbird*, he might say.

"And that's how we can all help lost owls feel at home in our barns and attics!" Sundae said as the slideshow ended. A few people applauded enthusiastically.

"What a sweet endearment," Sundae said dreamily, sitting down beside Dorothy. She kicked her sneakers back and forth.

Dorothy leaned close. "Is there anyone special in your life, Sundae?"

"Oh no." Sundae laughed. "I have lots of responsibilities. Plus I've lived in a swamp most of my life." She sipped her tea. "But I like love stories. And I adore love, all kinds of love. Sometimes I wonder what it might be like to find someone special like that. Like a best friend, but better."

Thea was fidgety-uncomfortable at the sound of Sundae talking about love. *Gross.* But the dreamy look in her sister's eyes was pretty cute.

The doors from the kitchen burst open, and the room was enveloped with the smell of warm sugar. Wendell pushed out a tray of small cakes, all swirled with different colors of icing.

"H-hello!" he said, peeking around the mountain of confections. "Happy birthday to m-me."

The ladies in the parlor all laughed and applauded.

"Good Gawd, darlin'." Bertha took in an eyeful

of the cakes. "How many cakes did you make?"

Thea helped Wendell distribute. "This is a Problim family birthday tradition—smash cake. You can't use your hands to eat it. We all sing 'Happy Birthday.' You make a wish. And then you smash your face into the cake."

"We make a wish?" Bertha asked. "But it's your birthday, ain't it?"

Thea shrugged. "We think wishes are for anybody brave enough to believe they might come true."

"Everybody come inside!" Sundae yelled. "Smash cakes are ready!"

Thundering footsteps echoed through the mansion as neighborhood kids crowded into the room.

Toot puffed a #227[21] to get everyone's attention. And then the birthday song rang out. Birthdays were special days for the Problim family—as important as any proper holiday. They shouted out the lyrics of the song, and the room was full of happy noise. All the kids in the neighborhood embraced the smash cake tradition. LeeLee went first, followed by Noah. Alabama Timberwhiff turned his hat backward and

---

21 #227: The Hushfart: Softer sounding than a referee's whistle, but still shrill. Smells like dirty clothes. Means: be quiet!

smash-caked at the same time as Mona.

The moms looked at their little cakes as if they were confused. But before anyone could ask a question, Mrs. Wong plunged in headfirst.

Noah, who was still in the process of wiping icing off his face, froze. "Did . . . my mom just do that?"

LeeLee nodded. "Uh-huh. And my mama's about to do it too. Go, Mama, go!"

LeeLee's mom had a wonderful, bubbly laugh, which erupted from her icing-covered face.

Bertha smash-caked next. Dorothy barely tapped her nose into the cake. Then she giggled. Mrs. Timberwhiff was the last to cake-smash. She tried to hold in her laughter, but it didn't work. She guffawed at the icing on her chin and the icing on her friends' faces.

Wendell and Thea cake-smashed at the same time, just like they had for the past twelve years.

"Happy Wednesday," she told him.

"Happy Th-Thursday," he replied.

But their days were getting different now. Instead of running away together to build an obstacle course or train circus spiders, Wendell ran for the kitchen to get more food. And Thea walked to the backyard with her shoulders slumped.

Eventually the kids migrated outside again. A small piece of cake was given to Ichabod, and Wendell had made a special peanut butter smash cake for Melody Larson's service dog, Xena.

As Thea watched the party from a distance, Toot waddled toward her, a #6[22] hovering around him. He pointed to the spider lady, who was walking up the sidewalk.

Thea scooped him up into her arms and ran to find Sal. But Sal was already halfway through the foyer, wearing goggles and carrying a foaming cauldron of punch.

"I smell a #6," Sal said. "What's up?"

Wendell, Mona, and Frida also ran into the foyer.

Sundae scampered out of the room of adults, who were having a country classics karaoke competition. "What's happening?"

The door opened slowly.

Toot grunted and narrowed his eyes.

Desdemona O'Pinion walked inside, flanked by Carley-Rue and Will.

---

22 #6: The Paul Revere: A trumpetous fart of warning. One toot if by land. Two toots if by sea. Smells of cruciferous vegetables.

"My invitation must have been lost in the mail." Desdemona smiled. "But it looks like I'm just in time! Found any proof that you're Problems yet?"

"Our parents are on their way," Sundae told her. Then she promptly changed the subject. "We're so happy to see you. Is Violet with you?"

"Violet?" Carley-Rue scoffed. "She never leaves her room."

"She's far too sick," Desdemona added. Her eyes narrowed. "Wait. How do you know Violet, anyway?"

"We heard the neighborhood kids talking about her," Sundae said quickly. "We were just asking who all we should invite. Violet's name came up."

"I'm sure." Desdemona smiled faintly. "Regardless, I am delighted to be here."

"Adults are in this room," Sundae said, ushering Desdemona toward the library. "We were just about to have a sing-along and group dance. Kids are in the garden for now."

Sal pushed the cauldron into Will's arms. "Take this with you and head through those doors."

"Now what do we do?" Thea asked. "Ms. O'Pinion wants the treasure."

"Why didn't she bring V-Violet?" Wendell wondered aloud.

"Stop asking about Violet," Thea huffed. She stared at the ground, at the adorable circus spider clinging to her shoelaces, so she didn't see the expression on her brother's face. She hated herself for not wanting him to be happy.

"Violet said they won't let her out of the house, remember?" Sal looked at Thea and Mona. "Any thoughts? We can't bail on the party to watch Desdemona O'Pinion. We've got to convince these people not to kick us out of their neighborhood."

"So we just need the O'Pinions to l-leave, then," Wendell suggested.

Mona rolled her eyes. "Don't worry. I'll handle them."

"No," Sundae said softly. "But I appreciate your enthusiasm."

"Wait!" Thea said, biting her lip as a plan unfolded. "I think we should let Ms. O'Pinion look."

Sal was already shaking his head, but Thea continued, "And we watch her. She's lived beside this house all her life. They've got binoculars hanging on every one of their windows so they can try to look inside. She may even know what it looked like when Grandpa lived here. What if she knows something we don't? What if she discovers a clue that was meant for us? What if she leads us to more bonesticks?"

Sal nodded. "That's actually a good idea, Thea."

Thea beamed. Wendell nodded at her. Thump, *bump*.

She'd missed that feeling.

Sal asked, "But even if Desdemona does go sneaking around, or sends her minions sneaking around, how do we keep an eye on her?"

"Every Problim be on the lookout," Sundae said. "And if she's on the move, we'll tell Toot. Toot sends another signal—"

Toot clapped.

Thea looked at Frida. "And then I think you should follow her. You're sneaky enough to go unnoticed. Just be careful, Frida. Try not to bump into anything."

Frida nodded excitedly. She pulled her fox hood up over her head and said:

*"The fox
Shall watch*

And lie in wait.
Protect her skulk
whatever it takes!"

Toot puffed a #104.

"A skulk is a family of foxes!" Sundae answered. "So clever, Frida! So we're all set?"

"Yes." Thea nodded. "For now, let's go enjoy our birthday party."

"This is getting c-complicated," Wendell said to Sal.

And Sal couldn't help but smile. "Actually . . . this is getting fun."

Wednesday/Thursday

Wendell showed the neighborhood kids the secret passage, even though Thea said it was off-limits. The Room of Constellations felt like hers, and she didn't like so many people in her secret dreaming space. She should be excited—she wanted to make friends. She should follow Wendell's lead.

Should, should, should, she thought. She should feel all kinds of things, probably. But all she really felt was lonely.

Midge Lodestar once said that if you want to start a conversation with someone, there was one surefire question that always made people want to talk to you.

So Thea stood up to her full height, took a deep breath, and approached a boy in the middle of the room wearing a Spider-Man T-shirt.

"Hello!" Thea smiled. "What's your favorite taco combo?"

The boy blinked and looked around like he needed help answering the question. "I . . . don't know?" He shrugged.

And that was that. She couldn't think of anything else to ask. So she nodded. "Right. Thanks."

Terrible! Thea dropped her head and leaned against a star wall. She wished she could disappear into those constellations. How could she be so bad at talking to other kids her age?

The neighbors seemed to like her room just fine—and they especially seemed to like that it was only accessible through a secret passage. Sal climbed the stairs up to the room behind Melody Larson, explaining the cool details about the house to her since she couldn't see them. Xena flanked her other side.

Several neighborhood children circled up in the front of the room and played a boring game they seemed to like. It was called charades.

"You're a mommy, pushing a baby carriage!"

someone yelled to LeeLee, who was the first to take a turn.

"No," Noah Wong yelled. "I know! You're the Widow Dorrie!"

Everyone cheered.

Thea had invited the widow to the party. But Dorrie still hadn't come by. And really, Thea didn't think she would. Maybe she didn't need a friend. Or maybe the widow didn't want to be Thea's friend.

Or maybe the widow just didn't like kids. Period. Mona didn't like kids either, and Mona *was* a kid.

A thought jumped suddenly into Thea's brain:

Where widows watch . . .

There was a widow in this town. What if that widow had a clue?

The witch will help, but you must lead . . .

Even if the widow wasn't really a witch, maybe she was still the one with helpful insight?

Thea wanted to tell Wendell this new idea, but he was eating snacks with some boys in the corner. So she turned to Mona (who was in the process of sticking a circus spider in someone's cup of punch) and babbled to her instead.

"Think about it, Mona! Dorrie would certainly have been here seven years ago before Grandpa left, right? And even if she wasn't here, maybe she could figure out the clues. She lives in a witchy cottage, apparently. And! She's a widow! I just need to know what she watches all day!"

The spider scrambled up Mona's arm. She groaned and grabbed its twitchy legs again. "She watches the baby, right?"

It wasn't a bad thought, actually. Maybe there was a clue in the baby carriage!

"I'll go find out!" Thea told Mona.

"Wendell's busy."

"I don't always have to take Wendell," Thea said. "I can do things alone too."

She wanted to take him, of course. Thea didn't love the idea of adventuring into dark woods all alone. She glanced toward Wendell just in time to see him laughing along with everyone else watching the charades game.

Wendell, she realized, was having his own adventures now. And Thea decided—half to make him mad, and half for reasons she didn't understand—that she wanted her own adventure too.

"Don't tell him where I'm going. I'll tell Frida so she can come and find me if I get lost."

Mona groaned again as the spider clung to her

finger. "You're leaving your own birthday party?"

Thea nodded. "I don't think I'm good at parties."

A clatter of feet clicked on the floor behind Thea. *Ork-ork*, Ichabod nudged her leg.

"I'll take Ichabod with me." She smiled. "Remember, keep an eye on—"

"The spider lady," Mona answered. A slow, sweet smile stretched across her face. "I'll take care of her."

Thea kneeled down and gave Ichabod a quick hug, then led him through the secret passage alone. She heard the echo of laughter behind her from the Room of Constellations—laughter getting farther and farther away. She walked through the library unnoticed and heard the neighborhood moms cooing over the food and the owl pictures and precious, funny little Toot. The room was full of cake-crumb smiles; they thought all his farts were charming.

"They won't even miss me, Ichabod," Thea said brightly. She didn't feel bright, but she tried to pretend. She lifted her chin high and walked out the front door heart-first. Ichabod trotted beside her as Thea grabbed her bicycle and walked it through the yard.

Ork-ork! The pig nudged her leg. Above them,

moonlight shimmered across the silvery webs of the circus spiders. Thea concentrated on new bubbles forming:

Thea, alone, against the wall of her room while other kids whispered and laughed about how awkward she was.

Thea, alone, while the rest of her siblings walked arm-in-arm with new friends.

"I'm . . . alone," Thea confirmed. Ichabod let out an angry *Ork!*

"I know. These are just rumors." Thea leaned down to pet the pig's soft ears. "I probably put them there myself. I don't like being by myself. Do you really think I can go see Dorrie . . . alone? What if I get scared?"

The pig oinked affirmatively.

"You're right." Thea nodded. "Every day is a good day for a taco."

Alone . . . and yet, she was determined to have an adventure anyway. Thea pushed off on the bike and wobbled down Main Street (It wasn't so easy to ride a tandem bike all alone!), toward the boundary of the Bagshaw Forest. Ichabod pranced beside her. Is this what brave feels like, Thea wondered. Midge Lodestar hadn't told her to do this. She'd just done it. Adventuring alone felt terrible, at first. But it also felt right. Like it needed to happen. Like it was time. She whistled Grandpa's song as she peddled:

"Tell me a tale worth telling back,

And I'll sing you a new song, clackity-clack."

Thea couldn't remember the first time she'd heard the song. But this was the first time she understood the meaning: she was making a story of her own. She was living her own adventure. She missed Wendell, to an infinite degree. But it's not like she couldn't tell him about it later.

She liked this feeling very much.

⟳

Wendell couldn't find his twin. It was their birthday, and she'd abandoned him somewhere. Twins for the win! . . . So much for that idea. He ran downstairs to the kitchen to replenish the tray of snacks. He swirled crackers with some sort of slimy, cheese-colored canned substance that Sal said the neighborhood kids liked to eat. And then he pulled more fresh raspberry macaroons from the oven.

That's when he smelled a #6[23] tangled in the air.

Wendell spun around just in time to see Desdemona O'Pinion sneaking up the staircase.

With a heavy tray of desserts balanced carefully in his arms, he followed her.

❦

"Guess what I am?" Frida shouted to the room of children. She growled, pounced on all fours, then shivered. But the kids kept talking loudly as if she wasn't there.

After many tries, her tiny shoulders drooped. "I'm an abominable snow fox," she said.

Mona walked over and patted her shoulder. "They have no imagination. I have a better game."

Frida tapped her chin, deep in thought.

"Sundae Problim would say no.
But the fox says yes.
The fox says GO!"

Mona clasped her hands together and smiled sweetly at the kids in the room. "Who's in the mood

---

23 #6: The Paul Revere: A trumpetous fart of warning. One toot if by land. Two toots if by sea. Smells of cruciferous vegetables.

for some real exploration?"

Wendell managed to duck behind the curved wall of the staircase just as Desdemona glanced back. When he peeked around the corner again, he saw her walk into one of the empty upstairs rooms. He took a step to follow. But something underneath the staircase grabbed his ankle. He dropped the tray of macaroons, and they clattered softly down the stairs.

"Not now, M-Mona!" he whispered angrily as he shook his sneaker loose from the sneaky prankster. The noise in the parlor paused momentarily, but then Sundae's guitar music filled the air again. Wendell bent down to drag his sister out, only to realize it wasn't Mona. It was Sal.

"Thank goodness it's y-you!" Wendell said. He leaned down closer to his brother. "Get up here! Sh-she just went upstairs!"

"I've been trying to follow her too," Sal said. "But she's so quiet!"

"How'd you get down there?"

Sal smiled. "There's a secret door behind the blackberry bush in the garden. Leads to this little closet room under the stairs. I found it when we moved in, but I've kept it secret. Because of Mona. You understand."

"Of c-course. So you can watch the enemy now?"

"I'm on it," Sal promised.

Wendell picked up the tray and tried to stand, but Sal grabbed his ankle again.

"Stop d-doing that!"

"Just one more thing!" Sal whispered. "Kick that macaroon a little closer so I can reach it."

By the time Wendell actually made it to the top of the stairs with only one shoe, Desdemona had disappeared from view. But a sparkle of light caught his eye from the house next door. It was Violet O'Pinion, sitting in her window. She wasn't wearing her helmet, probably because the air in her room was purified. She just watched the Problim house with her tiny face propped in her hands. Something about Violet's face reminded him of the girl in the book he was reading. *Alice in Wonderland*. Alice was like Violet; they both longed for adventure. Alice stepped through the looking glass to find adventure; Violet only wanted to go next door.

Besides, she deserved a smash cake. Every person deserves a smash cake.

Wendell tapped the glass and waved at Violet. She waved back, just once. Her tiny mouth tilted in a quick half grin.

Sal, Mona, and Frida could handle Desdemona, for a few minutes at least.

Wendell had another adventure in mind, and it involved the astronaut behind the glass.

The Widow in the Woods

Thea swung off her bicycle and pushed it past the boundary of the Bagshaw Forest. Her heart hammered a fearful warning inside her chest. She'd lived in the Swampy Woods most of her life. So why was she so terrified of these? The Bagshaw Forest was different than the Swampy Woods, for sure. It was darker. The trees were taller, and shadows seemed to move and bloom as fast as Sal's fog. Mostly though, she didn't like this forest because it didn't contain her siblings.

Thump . . . *bump.*

    Thump . . . *bump.*

Wendell's heartspeak was getting farther and farther away.

"I'm not like the rest of them," Thea told Ichabod. "I'm not adventurous. I'm only afraid. *Thursday's child has far to go.* That's the worst day of the week to be born on, you know? Sundae and Mona got the best ones. Full of wisdom. Fair of face. Smart. Beautiful. And . . . ugh."

Ichabod *ork-ork*ed. She scratched his soft head.

Thea followed a well-worn path through the woods; one that had been traveled plenty by four-wheelers, bikes, and hiking boots. She felt a little bit like a detective in one of Wendell's books.

"Do you think growing up means growing apart?" she asked the pig, as if he'd answer.

Silvery mist billowed off the leaf-covered ground.

"So dark in here," Thea whispered.

And for the first time she considered: What if the neighbors were right about the widow? What if the rumors were true? Maybe she didn't just live in a witchy cottage. Maybe she really was a witch!

Thea passed under a thick canopy of trees and saw a cottage with a thin spiral of smoke curling from the chimney. The garden surrounding the cottage was overgrown and wild. A little bit witchy, maybe. And as Thea got closer, she could see cages of live birds—predatory birds that didn't tweet sweetly, like Sundae's bluebirds. These birds screeched so loud and shrill that Thea's bones seemed to shiver at the sound.

"Ichabod, if this is like *Hansel and Gretel* and she's really a witch, you need to run away. And you need to figure out a way tell my siblings that I love them, okay?"

"I can tell 'em that if you want," came a raspy old voice from behind her. Thea spun around with a gasp.

The Widow Dorrie stood tall, her hands propped on her hips. She wore no straw hat today, just an old T-shirt, overalls, and mud boots up past her knees. Her hair was silver-white and wispy. Dorrie's face was wrinkled, but not in a witchy way. The Widow Dorrie had the kind of wrinkles that came from laughing and smiling and planting gardens in the sun. She wore the same look she'd had the other day; not a mean grin, but the kind of smirk like you're in on a joke.

And then there were the eyes: crystal blue and as sad as the last skies of summer. Dorrie was lonely. Dorrie had known loss. Thea didn't know how she knew those things, but she did. She'd always known what Wendell was feeling. That came easy. But it was different to feel connected to a stranger.

"I'm Thea." She didn't know what else to say. "I left the flower for you."

Dorrie shoved her hands in her pockets. "The one that smelled like a ripe old fart?"

"I promise it wasn't a prank," Thea insisted. "My brother thought a fart garden might keep our nosy neighbors away."

Dorrie nodded. "Well, that's a fine idea. Might try it myself. I don't have many neighbors out here, of course. But I got crows trying to eat my corn patch. They're not afraid of my scarecrows anymore."

And then Dorrie smiled outright, a toothy, beautiful grin that made Thea feel much less nervous. "You want to come inside, Thea? I couldn't attend your birthday party today; I'm not always in the mood to spend time around that bitter old hen that lives next door to you. But I do like a good cup of tea with a kindhearted soul. Free tea for the fearful, I always say." She smiled. "Plus, you can help me feed Morris."

Very gently, Dorrie pulled a bandanna bundle

from the pocket of her overalls. Inside was a baby rabbit that glanced around with watery, fearful eyes.

"He's so tiny!" Thea said. "Is it okay to pet him?"

"Sure." Dorrie smiled. "Just gently, now. He got in a tangle a few days ago, but he'll be faring better in no time. Come on in."

"I would love to come inside. But I have an important question I must ask you immediately—"

"Nope!" Dorrie waved her toward the door. "I only answer important questions over tea."

Thea looked down at Ichabod.

"The pig can come too!" Dorrie said.

Ichabod didn't need a second invite. He turned his face up happily and pranced into the cottage.

Dorrie's cottage was kind of pretty up close. It certainly wasn't the eyesore the MOOS made it out to be. It was small, with ivy climbing up the walls and little white flowers sparkling through all that green. And it was in the middle of a wild and lovely garden. Sal would love Dorrie's garden, Thea knew. It contained no funky dump-sculptures, like Sal enjoyed creating. But this garden still had a cool flow: full of wildflowers and tall purple lilacs that served as a resting spot for butterflies.

As Thea walked toward the door, she got a better look at the creatures in the cages too: a hawk with a bandage on its wing. A tiny wattabat with a patch over its middle eye. She even saw a crow with only one wing hopping around in a pen with a bunch of chickens.

Dorrie nodded to the crow. "He's fit in quite fine with his new family, don't you think? He's the odd one out, but they don't seem to care."

Thea locked eyes with the Widow Dorrie: they were both odd ones too. But Thea had always had six other weird siblings to lean on. Had Dorrie ever had someone? Or had she been alone all this time?

"Make yourself comfy," Dorrie encouraged, opening the door. "If a girl misses her own birthday party, she must have some pretty important questions. And I might have some answers . . ."

Wendell pushed the window open. He would use Mona's bow and arrow to shoot a zip line to Violet's chimney. He hoped he could launch and land where he was supposed to without breaking Violet O'Pinion's window. He'd done it plenty of times in the Swampy Woods, but not over much longer distances. The calculations couldn't be that hard.

It also occurred to him that he was leaving the neighborhood children alone with Mona. But that was as it had to be. Mona couldn't do anything too dreadful in the time it would take him to get back. Probably. Besides, if they got to stay in Number Seven, the neighborhood kids would have to protect themselves against Mona's schemes eventually.

∽

"I don't understand this game!" Noah Wong called out from behind the door of the dark room.

"You have to get used to it," Mona said, leaning against the other side. "My siblings and I play 'Try to Get Out of This Room' all the time."

A short silence. And then Noah replied, "That does not sound like fun."

"It's a riot," Mona mumbled to herself.

Carley-Rue banged her fist on the door. "I need my mom."

"Your mom's busy snooping," Mona said.

"Why can't you just push a key under the door?" Alabama Timberwhiff asked.

"But that's so easy!" Mona moaned. "Don't you want to figure out how to pick the lock?"

Frida jumped down from the bookshelf in the hall and shook her head at Mona, saying:

"'Try to Get Out of This Room' is always fun,
but the neighbors don't know how it's done."

Mona shrugged. "They'll learn. If they're not out
in a few hours, we'll send in the spiders to make it
more interesting."

Mona walked away whistling.

And Frida pounced up to the second floor, where
she'd seen Sal going earlier. Frida said:

"Sal is brave!
Sal is quick!
He'll free the captives in a single click!"

Frida's sneakers screeched to a stop when she saw
Desdemona snooping. Frida said:

"Oh no!
Oh dear!
The fox forgot!
I won't let the enemy win.
I WILL NOT!"

Sal had turned one of the upstairs rooms into
an indoor greenhouse, and that's where the spider

lady was stooped down, searching behind a giant orchid. Quickly, Frida pounced into the room, sliding behind a miniature palm tree. She pumped her arm in victory . . . and accidentally knocked over a flowering cactus. The cactus pot shattered.

Desdemona whirled around. "Who's there?"

Frida was good at making herself invisible. She held her breath in the dark corner, sucked in her belly, and tried to make herself as flat and still against the wall as possible. Desdemona inched closer. Frida was sure she'd be discovered at any second. Just as Desdemona took a last step that might reveal Frida outright, a familiar, clinking metallic sound echoed in the hallway.

"Are you lost?" Sal asked as he stepped into the room.

"I was looking for the restroom."

"It's not in here with my plants."

Desdemona took a step toward him, and Sal pulled his shears. He quickly snipped a spider's web that was dangling from Desdemona's sweater. But Desdemona jumped backward, as if he'd intended to hurt her. She gave him a wide circle as she made her way for the door. "I'll find it on my own."

As they heard Desdemona's steps rumbling down

the hallway, Frida finally called out to her brother in a fearful whisper.

"What are you doing in here?" Sal said, pulling her out from behind the corner. "Are you hurt?"

Frida replied:

"No, I wasn't!
I was looking for you!
Downtrodden!
Perplexed!
I don't know what to do!
We have a problem.
A Problim problem."

"Mona Problim?" Sal asked.

"That's the one!" Frida nodded.

"Where's Wendell?"

Frida said:

"He's gone to get Violet,
And Thea's adventuring.
This party's a riot!"

Sal pushed his hand through his hair. "We can't watch Mona *and* follow the spider woman!" Sal was a quick thinker. He soon came up with the perfect plan. "Okay. We'll lock Mona in the broom closet until the party is over."

Frida grimaced and said:

"If you do that,
Her revenge will be brisk.
Don't do it, Sal.
It's not worth the risk."

Sal shrugged. "She's always plotting something terrible for me anyway. Go get Fiona the Flytrap and put her in the closet. And leave a cupcake or something in there too. For Fiona. Tell Mona you saw a rat skeleton in the closet so she'll go look inside. We'll lock her in there. We'll get the neighborhood kids out of the room. Then we can focus on Desdemona again. I'm depending on you, Fox."

Frida zipped up her fox hoodie so the ears atop her head were super pointy. She responded:

"I won't let you down.
I'm a fox on a mission!
I'll go get the flytrap
and secure my position!"

Violet O'Pinion had spent most of the afternoon watching people arrive for the party she couldn't attend. She at least wanted Biscuit, her tiny fluffball of a dog, to go. She let her dog out and watched her prance around the Problim yard with the other neighborhood dogs, until it got too dark. Then Biscuit had become obsessed with digging near a camellia bush beside the gate. The dog had something long and white in her mouth as she scampered back to Violet's house.

Did she find a *bone*? Violet wondered.

Biscuit shook off in the decontamination doggy hallway, passed through the detox door, and then pounced into the room. She pranced around with the stick in her mouth as if she'd been playing fetch. Violet grinned as she took the stick and reared back to toss it across the room.

But then she realized that it wasn't like other sticks—it felt heavy. And it looked different up close. Twiggy and white—almost like a bone—with strange, golden edges. She put it in a flower pot, filled it with dirt, and watered it. She imagined it sprouting leaves someday.

"This is a hard place to bloom," Violet said to

the plant. She loved the sound of her voice without the helmet. Her room was the only place in the world she didn't have to wear it; the air was perfectly controlled. And her dog was hypoallergenic, both thanks to her dad. He'd do anything for her, she knew that. And she knew he only wanted to keep her safe.

But Violet was the kind of girl who couldn't stop her heart from dreaming, and dreaming is so rarely a safe occupation. The most obvious proof was her walls: she'd covered them in maps of the world. Her father had painted her room pink, but since Violet had never really liked the color pink she covered the walls with pages from atlases and maps—old ones, new ones, storybook maps even. She had so many maps, there wasn't a spot of pink left.

She looked at those worlds constantly. And she dreamed.

She dreamed of doing cartwheels on the Great Wall of China.

She dreamed of having high tea with the princess of England and then playing soccer beside the Thames. And riding gondolas in Italy. And being a cowgirl in Montana. And what it might feel like to stand on the edge of the Rocky Mountains and shout her name into the vast, blue, beautiful world. Without a helmet. Without anything holding her back.

And while dreaming gave her comfort, it had never helped her leave her tower.

Not until the other day, when the fog out the window bloomed like roses and animals, and she couldn't stand being inside anymore. That was the first time she had ever snuck outside; because she was desperate to meet the new neighbors. The Problim children.

Violet had taken one stickpin from her desk. She carefully plotted it on one of the maps of her own neighborhood. One hundred feet from her front door—that had been her first adventure.

And she hoped it would not be her last.

THOMP!

Biscuit *yap-yap-yapp*ed, high pitched and fierce.

Violet spun toward her window.

"Shh," Violet said, picking up the dog and cradling it in her arms. "We're okay."

Balancing on the ledge was one of the Problim children—the boy with the kind eyes and sideways glasses. He smiled. And waved. Violet waved back.

"You're missing the p-party," Wendell said, his

breath fogging the other side of the glass. He pointed to his zip line attached to the chimney. "But I came to offer you a ride."

Violet smiled. She put down the dog and went to hide the funny tree in her closet again. "Sleep well," she said to the tiny plant.

She snapped her helmet in place and ran for the window, still smiling as she opened it. She couldn't stop with the smiling. She smiled so hard her face nearly hurt as Wendell helped her hold on to the zip line.

"Push off when you're ready," he said. "Then send it back over. You'll love it—it feels just like fl-flying."

Flying. She was flying; and she squealed in total delight.

Sometimes dreams do come true, Violet realized. Because she was already off on her second adventure.

Midge Lodestar

Thea was surprised to find the sunflower she'd left for Dorrie still blooming in the old woman's cottage. Dorrie had cut off half the stem and settled it in a mason jar on the center of her small table. Thankfully, the flower no longer smelled like a #297.[24]

Dorrie's cottage was cozy and filled with comfy chairs and scattered books. Several lamps were on, and a few candles flickered over the fireplace. A tiny raccoon slept in a hammock draped in one of the windows, snoring happily.

---

24 #297: The Violent but Deadly: Toot Problim's worst contribution to the atmosphere by far, this particular toot contains notes of sewage and skunk spray and can linger for up to two hours.

"That's Reggie," Dorrie said, settling a cup of tea in front of Thea. "He's the one I was walking in the carriage the day I passed y'all at the playground. Reggie got stuck in a hunter's trap. He's healing fine, but he's too nervous to make his way in the world just yet. So I take him for walks. Let him snooze or look around or just breathe in the air; whatever it takes to get reacquainted with the world."

"I love animals too," Thea said. "My family has a pet pig. And circus spiders."

"Circus spiders!" Dorrie grinned. "They're a hoot."

"Yes! They're very well trained. And my sister has a Venus flytrap . . . if you consider that a pet."

The room smelled like warm caramel-apple muffins, which Dorrie pulled from the stove and plopped, still steaming, onto mismatched saucers.

"So you go first," Dorrie said. "Ask me your question."

Thea tried to give Dorrie a short version of everything that had transpired since they'd moved in to House Number Seven. "And then there's our terrible neighbor, Desdemona."

Thea noticed Dorrie stiffen—just slightly—at the sound of that name. But Thea kept going. "She thinks Grandpa stole a treasure from her family and hid it in the house. But no one has been allowed in the house, not even her. We think he meant for us to find the treasure, but Desdemona is going to throw us out. She even founded some horrible society for unwanted children—it's like she knew we would come. Even before we knew."

Dorrie sipped her tea. Thea could see the thought lines forming on the woman's forehead.

"Grandpa left us this riddle," Thea continued. "And that's fun! But we also need to prove we are Problims—and fast! And we need our parents to come home. So I thought you could help, maybe. I thought you could tell me what . . . widows watch. I hope that doesn't sound offensive."

"I'm not offended," Dorrie said as she sipped her tea. "I mostly watch *Jeopardy*."

"Oh." Thea nodded. "Okay, then. I hope you won't be offended by this either. The clue told us that a witch would help us find the treasure. And I heard someone say that you might be, a, you know . . ."

"I'm no witch," she added bluntly. "But I wish I was. I'd make my garden grow faster."

Thea sighed. "Oh."

"That said." Dorrie grinned over the rim of

the teacup. "There is another thing I like to watch: water. Oceans and rivers in particular. I could tell you more about why." Dorrie smiled kindly. "But it's too sad a story."

"Then you should definitely tell me," Thea assured her. "Especially if it makes it a little less sad for you. Besides, I don't mind sadness. My brother thinks sadness is a beautiful emotion."

"Okay, then. Follow me." Dorrie led Thea to the upstairs of the house, into a room that looked like an office. Two french doors opened to a tiny porch, overlooking the marshes. A three-legged cat slept on top of a bookshelf. The desk against the wall was stacked with radio equipment and headphones.

"This is where I do my real job, up here. I broadcast," Dorrie told her. "And over here is—"

"Wait a minute!" Thea's wild heart fluttered. It felt like finding a buried treasure! She beamed as she read an award tacked to Dorrie's wall: a Certification of Excellence for Midge Lodestar's radio program. "Do you know Midge Lodestar?"

Dorrie flung her arms open wide. "Darlin', you are *looking* at Midge Lodestar. That's my professional name."

"No way! I listen to your advice all the time! The

taco mantra helps me overcome all anxieties!"

"The . . . taco mantra?" Dorrie asked.

"Every day is a good day for a taco!"

Dorrie doubled over laughing. "Here's what's happened, darling. You see this map on the wall? I can only broadcast my show in this vicinity here." Dorrie waved her hand around the town of Lost Cove.

"But out in the Swampy Woods," she said, pointing to the inky tangle of trees showing Thea's old home. "You're only getting bits and pieces of what I say. That taco mantra? What you're hearing is a commercial for Hillary's Taco Truck, downtown in the Cove. You just got the jingle scrambled."

Thea felt embarrassed. She flopped down in the chair and sighed. "I scramble lots of things."

"Like what?"

"Making friends—that's an easy thing for everybody else. Probably because all of my siblings are unique and cool in some weirdly wonderful way and I try to be too, but I'm just ugh." Thea shrugged. "We're a perfect seven, you see. And from the time we were babies our mama sang that old nursery rhyme—the one about the days of the week. Everybody's day pretty much tells the truth about who they are. My twin, Wendell, he's always full of woe.

Not woe like 'woe is me,' but more like *whoa*! He's amazed by everything."

Dorrie grinned. "I'm familiar with that rhyme."

Thea's shoulders slumped. "And I never get anything right. I'm Thursday. I have far to go."

"Oh, I don't know about that," Dorrie said. "Every person's more than just one thing. Wendell's not just full of woe, is he? He's full of all kinds of things. The same's true of you." Dorrie smiled softly. "And it's true: you should never doubt the power of a taco." She laughed. "So do you want to see where this widow watches?"

"Yes!"

Dorrie pointed to the porch. It looked exactly the same as the Porch of Certain Death, but far less likely to fall and break into a billion pieces at the slightest toot.

Dorrie opened the door.

Thea took two baby steps toward her. She didn't want to tell Dorrie how much she hated heights. Dorrie was Midge Lodestar! She had to be brave for Midge! Besides . . . Thea really wanted to hear this story. If she could figure out the clue, at least she'd feel like she was something special in her family of exceptionals.

But each step she took was agony. When she walked out on the porch, Thea wondered if she might pass out. Or throw up. Or both. That'd be so embarrassing.

So she kept her eyes closed as Dorrie talked.

"I was widowed when I was twenty-one years old," Dorrie said. "I grew up on the coast, and my love was a sailor. I was the only thing he ever loved more than the sea. He was a fisherman; there were plenty of fishermen in my town. So folks would put porches like this out from the top of their house— a watch. Sometimes, folks call them a 'walk.' We would walk out on them every morning and watch for our sailors to come home. I used to stand on that porch—the one around our house—and watch for him to come back to me every night. You follow?"

"Yes, ma'am," Thea said. She smelled the woods. She could feel the ocean wind blowing warm over her face. Begging her to open her eyes. To see the beauty down below. She wanted to look. But couldn't.

"Well, one night, he took out his boat and got caught in a terrible storm. The boat made it home eventually, but my sailor did not."

Thea opened her eyes then to look at Dorrie, whose gaze settled over the marshlands. Dorrie didn't cry as she told the story, but Thea could hear and see a sadness there. She wondered if it was possible for tragedy to reshape a person's face, to forever change a smile, an outlook, and the way someone sees the world.

"Wouldn't you know, this funny little house where I ended up also has a watch on top! So sometimes I stand up here, and I watch way over there—where the river used to be." She laughed.

"What happened to the river?" Thea asked.

"That's a story for another time," Dorrie said softly. "Anyway, that's what this widow watches. The place where the river used to be. And I think about the life I used to live."

Thea sighed. "That's a sad story. And a beautiful story too. But I don't think my grandpa's clue had anything to do with the river. I wish it did, though. Thank you for trying to help."

"Sure, sure. Before you go, I've got a present for you! And I have a question. Wait right here."

"Right here? On the porch?" Thea said anxiously. "What if I wait in Midge Lodestar's office?"

"Just wait right there!" Dorrie said, disappearing back down the stairs.

Thea squeezed her eyes shut tight.

She heard the flutter of bird's wings. Then the tiny sound of bird's feet, pattering across the rail she gripped. The bird began singing a soft lullaby, as if it had shown up just to calm her.

That birdsong settled Thea's soul, and she opened her eyes.

First she saw the ravine—the place where the town river used to be. Past that, she saw a tall, rippled mountain. Somewhere close there was an ocean. And past that, a whole other world. It was overwhelming, just the thought of that much beauty. Suddenly, her hands weren't gripping the rails so tightly. She was leaning toward that wild world, propping her elbows on the rail, resting her face in her hands, without her usual fear of being pulled toward the ground.

In fact, her fear was giving way to something better: something like joy. Pure, perfect joy. And she never would have felt that if she hadn't been brave enough to venture on her own.

Dorrie climbed the stairs again and presented a tiny gift to Thea: a sunflower pin. The middle part was knitted from brown yarn, with black felt petals and a safety pin on the back. "You seem to love those dark flowers. So I wanted to make you one that wouldn't spoil. Or stink. Happy birthday, Thea Problim."

Thea pinned it to her collar. "I'll wear it every day!"

Dorrie smiled. "My sailor used to always bring me a red rose, from the time he courted me to the day he left. We were only married a short time, but each day, he'd come in and bring me a single red rose and say, 'I love you, and I need you, and I'll always come back for you.'"

"I'm sorry he didn't come back," Thea said. She'd tucked her hand into the crook of Dorrie's elbow without realizing it.

Dorrie shook her head. Her eyes were glassy with tears, but none fell. "And he was telling the truth, I believe. Someday when I'm even older than I am now, when it's my time to go, I think he'll come back for me. He'll have a rose pinned to his coat pocket and he'll tuck another behind my hair, and we'll dance the cha-cha right through glory's gates. I think we'll see each other again."

"One more thing before I go," Thea said. "You said you had a question for me?"

Midge nodded. "What do you think of your neighbors, the O'Pinions?"

"Desdemona O'Pinion is extra creepy." Thea said.

"The feud you hear so much about was between Mr. O'Pinion and your grandpa. If your granddad took something from the town, he took it for a good reason, not because he was some greedy thief who wanted it for himself. He was never selfish. Unfortunately, the same can't be said for Stan O'Pinion, Desdemona's dad. He's probably the one pushing Desdemona's buttons."

"He's still alive?" Thea asked.

"Oh yes," Dorrie nodded. "Alive and rotten as ever. And still scheming—wherever he is. You can be sure of that. Frank and Stan were best friends when they were boys. But the Great Feud tore those two apart."

"Grandpa's best friend betrayed him?" Thea asked sadly.

Dorrie nodded. "Best friends do that—and family too—when treasure is involved. And Stan became a bitter recluse after that. I know your grandpa was a good man, though. He was a dreamer. He was a wild adventurer. He believed in living all the days of his life. And if that's what folks claim is mad, well—then I think madness is a fine way to be remembered, don't you? So be vigilant, Thea Problim. The O'Pinions are vicious."

The Fox Prevails

Frida creeped down to the first floor and watched from behind a bookshelf as Desdemona moved around the library slowly, nervously tapping her finger against her chin. She murmured the names of the books quickly, scanning as though she were looking for something specific.

"Another old witch the color of bone," Desdemona mumbled as she glanced around the room.

Frida shivered. A witch! Just like the clue! Was a witch hidden in this library? Were they imprisoned here? Stuck in the pages of a book? This was getting far more dangerous than the Fox had anticipated!

"Ha!" Desdemona shouted. She pulled a dusty old book from the shelf. The cover was purple and velvety and something was embedded there. But what? Desdemona tried to pry the thing loose with her long fingernails. But it wouldn't budge. "Is this it?" Desdemona mumbled. "Why is it stuck?"

But it wasn't a witch, Frida realized. It was a bone-stick!

Desdemona gave up. She flipped through the book to see if anything else was stuck inside. Then she shook it, hard, to see if anything might fall out. Frida's face scrunched in anger as she watched the pages flap and flutter. Wendell would not tolerate someone treating books that way.

"Maybe Daddy can get the witch loose," Desdemona mumbled, looking at the cover again. She flung the book on the desk.

"Hey," Will said from the door, his CosmicMorpho 3030 Mask pushed up in his hair. "I can't find anything. I can't even find Carley-Rue."

Shoot, Frida thought. *The kids had been snooping around too!* Will had, at least. Carley-Rue was still locked upstairs.

"There's one here," Desdemona whispered. "It's

possible those swamp brats found the rest and hid them again, but they're here. Daddy said that old idiot broke the witch into pieces and hid it. How do we find the rest?" She paged through the book quickly, scanning for clues. But there were none. "Stupid man!" Desdemona snorted. "How typical of Frank Problim to glue the witch to the front of his own book!"

The witch?

The fox twitched.

But it was just an old stick!
Why on earth had the enemy called it a witch?

Will took the book from his mother and flipped the pages. "Looks like boring junk to me. But if Grandpa wants it, you should take it."

Frida had had enough. She refused to let the O'Pinions take any book from this library. If they wanted to borrow the book, that'd be different, but they didn't seem like the borrowing type. She reached to the nearest shelf, grabbed a heavy bookend, and threw it down hard on the floor. Desdemona shrieked, and Will jumped. The book fell from his arms, and Frida dived for it.

"What in the . . . what is happening?" Will shouted, backing against the wall.

Ha-ha! Frida thought:

The fox was so stealth
so sharp
and slick
that nobody could even see her trick!

Desdemona pushed off the bookcase and ran for the book. "Will! Shut the door!"

"Gladly," Will shouted, slamming the door as he ran out of the room.

Frida shoved open the window. "SAL!" she screamed, and slung the book outside as far as she could. Even though she'd tossed hard . . . the book didn't land very far away.

Desdemona hurdled through the window.

Too bad we're only on the first floor, Frida thought as her assailant landed on the ground with a heavy thud. Desdemona grinned gleefully and clapped her hand down on the book.

She stood, beaming, and ran her fingernails over

the cover. "Frank Problim and his funny little magic tricks. His funny little secrets. Daddy will know how to find the treasure."

Frida shouted:

"It's not your treasure,
you villainous clown!
Throw it back right now,
or the fox comes down!"

But Desdemona totally ignored her. Frida thought:

Was it a secret?
A story?
A chest full of gold?
What wonderful secrets did this old mansion
*   hold?*

Frida tried to pull herself over the window to pounce. Desdemona O'Pinion was about to have a clever Problim on her hands (or on her shoulders)!

But then a long, green twist of ivy snapped around Desdemona's ankle and pulled her to the ground. She dropped the book.

"What was that?" Desdemona shouted as she crab-crawled backward.

Sal's Wrangling Ivy wrapped around the book and pulled it in a quick streak back through the yard. Back to Sal, who was watching from underneath a tree.

He picked up the book, dusted it off, and thanked the ivy. "I believe this belongs to us," he said as he glared at Desdemona.

Desdemona jumped to her feet. "Your family and its dark, terrible magic. It's time to end all that." She stomped away. "Rue Baby! Will! We are leaving. *Now.*"

As she stomped away, Sal looked back at the library window, where a tiny pair of pointy orange ears peeked over the sill. "Well done, Fox," he said, with a salute and a smile.

⁓⁓⁓

The doorbell rang at the Problim mansion, which gave Sundae a quick reprieve from her guests. She was grateful for the break. Toot was a much better host anyway. The guests were having a ball, but Sundae's voice was rusty now from leading sing-alongs. She opened the door, expecting another lady from the neighborhood.

Instead, she found a boy about her age.

"Oh," he said. "Hey."

She blinked as if he might disappear. When she thought about neighborhood children, it hadn't occurred to her that there might also be a neighborhood teenager. Or that he might be quite adorable. "Hello."

The boy's hair was black and pulled back. He wore a hoodie, jeans, and scuffed up sneakers. He held up his phone. "Listen, this is really embarrassing, but I'm Alex Wong. Noah's brother."

"Right!" she said a little bit too excitedly. Then she frowned. "Why's that embarrassing? I adore the name Alex. Alexander the Great!"

His cheeks flushed. "More like Alexander the Mediocre."

Sundae smiled again. "There are lots of great Alexes. Conquerors, explorers, kings, wrestlers!"

"Actually, I don't mean my name is embarrassing." He grinned. "I mean the reason I'm *here* is embarrassing. Thing is . . . Noah called and said he's stuck in a room." Alex grinned sheepishly. "He's a dork. He can't help it. I don't know how it happened."

"We're all dorks around here," Sundae said. "And I have a feeling he got stuck there because of my sister. Long story. Just follow me. Oh!" She whirled on him just as he was about to step inside. "I'm Sundae."

"Like the day of the week?"

"Born on the day of the week." She smiled. "Spelled like the ice cream."

Alex smiled. "Cool." And then his face froze as he heard his mother laugh in the other room. "Listen, Sundae, if we could bypass my mom, that would be super."

So they snuck up the staircase, just in time to see Sal pick the lock of the room with his needle-nose pliers.

"Congrats," Sal shouted to the room as he reattached the pliers to his sleeve. "You all win."

Carley-Rue ran out first, yelling for her mom.

"She left already!" Sal hollered after her.

"Aww, we were so close to getting out on our own!" Noah said. "Another hour and we'd have had it!"

Noah high-fived his brother. "Thanks for coming, Alex! I tried to pick the lock like you said, but I'm just not good at it . . ."

Sal shrugged. "I can teach you to pick a lock. Or my sister Thea can. She's amazing with locks."

"Yeah? Great! Thea seems cool." Noah smiled.

He looked up at his brother. "I guess I'll stay until Mom leaves, then?"

"Glad you found a way out, dude." Alex ruffled his brother's hair. And then he looked at Sundae. It was just a glance, just a second when their eyes locked. All he said was, "See you around, Ice-Cream Sundae?"

But it made Sundae feel as happy as springtime in the swamp. Like that moment when little yellow mud-roses burst up through the mushy ground after a long winter. "Hope so, Alex the Great," she whispered back.

Sal chuckled as Alex left. "He made you blush."

She gave him a playful push. "Desdemona left."

Sal grinned. "I noticed. I'll take over games up here then," Sal told her. "Mona is . . . busy."

"Remember," Sundae said as she made for the stairs. "Normal games. Not Problim fun."

"Of course." Sal nodded. And then he turned to his guests and smiled. "Now if you'll follow me back outside, I'll show you our circus spiders!"

Elemental

Violet followed Wendell around Thea's Room of Constellations. For the first time, she really did feel like an astronaut. "If my aunt sees me here, I'll get in big trouble. She'll ground me forever."

"Which means you'd stay in your room like you always d-do?"

Violet grinned. "True."

Wendell showed Violet the riddle. She mumbled one section aloud:

"Mr. Biv will show the way,
Where widows watch is where he stays.

Nestled there inside the beast,
Is the first clue for which you seek."

Violet's eyes danced with an idea.

Sal walked in just as Wendell shouted, "B-brilliant!"

"What's brilliant?" Sal held up the purple book. "I need to talk to you about something."

"It can wait. I think Violet cracked part of the clue!"

Violet nodded proudly. Her voice crackled again through the speaker of her helmet. "Mr. Biv—Roy G. Biv—that's seven letters for all the colors in a rainbow: red, orange, yellow, green, blue, indigo, and violet—like me!"

"Of course it's seven letters," Sal said with a laugh. He tucked the book against his side. He was fairly certain he could trust Violet O'Pinion. But still . . . she was an O'Pinion. He didn't want to give too much away just yet.

"So now we look for rainbows." Violet smiled.

Sal nodded. "That sounds like something Sundae would suggest. When we first moved in, the sun made rainbows down in the library. They were all over the place, though . . ."

Violet applauded. "Then let's go look!"

~~~

As Thea pedaled back to the front door, guests were leaving. She ditched her bike behind the gate and jumped behind a large sculpture. Ichabod crouched beside her. She assumed people would be leaving angry.

But the guests were actually smiling. Laughing, even.

Mayor Wordhouse was still wiping icing from his face. Someone high-fived him for his extra spin down the stair slide. Mr. Larson was red-faced with laughter. His clothes were wet, and soapy suds clung to his face like a Santa beard. Melody walked beside him, and told her dad (and her dog, Xena) everything she'd loved about the Problim children.

"They're funny!" she said. "And really weird but in a good way. And when you're around them, you feel like it's okay to be weird too."

"Around here, it's fine to be a freak," Noah said.

Alabama wiped a swipe of icing off his forehead and licked it. "And it's okay if you aren't a freak too.

Like, you can just be kind of quiet and boring and it's still okay."

"You're not boring," Noah told him. "Then again, maybe everybody's kind of boring compared to the Problims . . ."

THOMP.

Thea heard the human catapult release.

"WAHHH!"

And Thea saw Bertha arch through the air, screaming with joy. The parachute popped, and Bertha laughed. She made double peace signs as she floated down to the ground.

"They have done a lot with the house," Mrs. Wong said, draping her arm around Noah's shoulders. "It reminds me of the stories I've heard the mayor tell about how the Problim mansion used to be."

Noah nodded and looked back. "They really aren't so bad."

Mrs. Timberwhiff was still eating her cake with a fork as she walked away. "I'm not convinced I want them as neighbors. But at least none of us died terrible deaths while inside. I really need the name of their caterer."

Inside, Thea heard Wendell and Sal talking in the

library. She ran in and found Sal, Wendell . . . and Violet.

"Oh," Thea said as the little astronaut whirled around.

Violet beamed. "You're Thea! Hi!"

Thea waved shyly.

"Th-there you are!" Wendell said. "Where've you been? V-Violet might have an idea about the clue."

Thea's heart sank a little bit. "Great."

"The clue has to do with rainbows," he told her. "Sometimes all the glass in this house catches the l-light and makes rainbows."

"But," Violet's crackly voice added, "if it's in a clue, the rainbow must be pretty obvious. Pretty big."

"Wait!" Thea pulled Theodora Problim back out from the corner and tried to position her the same way she'd been when they first arrived. "This statue was here in the library the first day we came, and Sal moved it. Because it reflected too much light, which gave him a happiness headache. I don't remember where Grandpa used to have it exactly. But on the first day, her lantern made a rainbow path! Do you remember? If we can remember exactly where Theodora was standing . . ."

Thea twisted the Theodora back and forth, but there was no sunlight to catch.

Sal sighed. "Should we break it? See if the treasure is inside Theodora's lantern?"

"No!" Thea said, suddenly protective of Theodora and her light. "Besides, the clue also says it's where widows watch. And widows watch the ocean. And *Jeopardy*."

Violet giggled at Thea's joke. Which made Thea smile, just a little.

"So . . . we're still s-stumped," Wendell said.

They stood in silence until someone began banging on a distant door. "Let. Me. OUT. Or bring me another cupcake, at least. I'm hungry. And maybe a fly for Fiona? And Sal, you *will* pay."

"Oops. That reminds me," Sal said. "I locked Mona in the closet while we had company. I'll go get her in a sec. First, look at this. This is the book Desdemona tried to 'check out' from the library. There's a bone-stick in the cover! And . . . Frida says Desdemona was calling it a witch."

Thea's eyebrows scrunched together in concentration. "I don't understand."

"I don't either," Sal admitted. "But I did a quick scan of the library and found this . . ." He held up another book with a hole in the cover. "I think there was a bone-stick here too. Grandpa said there were three in the library, remember?"

Thea's heart sank. "But how will we find it now? Where did it go?"

"I . . . don't know. But check out the authors of the books."

The Seven Ancient Elements by Frank Cornelius Armadillo Problim and . . .

"Theodora Problim!" Thea yelled. "She's the statue girl! She was a Thursday, and she was a leader, and . . . she was an author!"

The other book, also written by Frank and Theodora, was called *Rare and Fabulous Plants of the Carolinas.*

"Grandpa was an author too, apparently." Sal passed the books to Wendell. "You're the mega-reader. Want to skim it and see if you find anything?"

Wendell nodded. Thea noticed her twin's hand shaking a little when he took the book. She could feel the anxiety there. Maybe because there could be important clues hidden in those pages. Or because they'd found another bone-stick. But also, more likely, because Wendell was overwhelmed holding something that belonged to his grandfather. Because it was another book shared between them.

Thump, *bump. It's okay,* Thea heartspoke. *You've got this.*

She waited a steady second. Thump, *bump.* And Wendell's heart—and the heart of his twin—settled into something more like excitement.

The Wishing Captain

Thea stood behind Sal as he opened the closet door, which emitted a long, low squeak. The flytrap was still in there. Mona was not.

"Oh no." Thea shook her head. "She found a way out. Now she'll come for you."

Thea saw her brother swallow visibly. "But there is no way out!" He stepped into the closet to grab the flytrap. "It's a closet, not a passage—" Sal grabbed his flashlight and held it out like a sword. "Mona!" he called. "Reveal yourself!"

With a wild scream, Mona jumped down from the top of the closet—eyes shining, arms spread wide. She looked like a deadly—but beautiful—zombiefreak,

Thea thought. Sal's own scream of terror ended quickly when Mona slammed into him.

"Fiona needs a snack," Mona said as she stood, narrowing her eyes at Sal. "Next time you put me in a closet, I'll feed her your fingers. One by one."

Sal's voice was muffled by the floor. "I might as well search this closet again for a clue while I'm in here." He pulled a magnifying glass from his belt. "Go check on Wendell, Thea?"

Wendell-Thea. Wendell-Thea. Maybe people did say that a lot.

After sending Violet back across the zip line (she insisted on going alone), Wendell had zoomed back to the library to look for more clues. He looked most relaxed among the books, Thea thought. That was his happy place, his perfect world. He'd tucked into the corner of a plush old couch holding Frank Problim's books.

Thea sat down beside him, curling her legs up pretzel-style in the seat. Wendell passed her a bag of popcorn he'd been munching on—a spicy chocolate flavor he'd concocted for the party. He was speed-reading, but other than a few "hmms" or an "oh . . . cool!" he hadn't found anything worth sharing yet.

Sundae sorted party leftovers on bookshelves, using the Dewey decimal system to organize each snack. "Chocolate cookies in section 398.2—the fairy tales! Because wouldn't it be fun to live in a castle made of cookie dough? I think so! And these wontons belong in the mystery section. Because I don't know what's inside them and they smell . . . like dead fish, a little."

With a grunt, Toot tapped his tiny heel against Ichabod's side, and they rode over to Sundae. The baby farted a squishy #14[25] as he took one.

"I made those," Mona said, marching back into the room.

Sundae slapped the wonton out of Toot's hand. "Let's move them to the horror section, then. Hello, treasure hunters! Anybody need a snack? I'll go get the rest, then I'll be back!"

Frida applauded Sundae's rhyme.

"There's no treasure here to hunt besides these sticks," Thea said. "We've already looked every-where. Unless Wendell finds a new clue in the book or proof that we're Problems . . . we're sunk."

---

25 #14: The Bon Appétit: Mellow smell of the kitchen after cooking stinky fish. Released when Toot is ready to enjoy a delicious meal.

"I'm w-working on it!"

Thea stared at Theodora's statue as if she might have some answers about the treasure Grandpa had stolen. *Hidden*, she thought. He would not steal a thing. Sal still thought they should smash the statue. Or at least break it in two. He even tried to coax Frida closer to it, so she might knock it over "accidentally" and he could see if the treasure was inside.

"Now here's s-something," Wendell said, tapping a page from the book about plants. "There's a rare tree that used to grow in Lost Cove called a Wondering W-Willow Birch—white bark, like a birch tree. But it only grows near water. The branches have been dowsing rods."

"Cool!" Sal cried, grabbing the book from his brother. "I've read about those!"

Thea sighed. "Will someone tell me what it is?"

"A dowsing rod finds water," Sal said. "And this tree here . . . the book says it's a legendary tree, that there were stories of dowsing rods leading the adventurer to enchanted rivers. Think Grandpa went looking for one?"

"Or," Thea said, leaning close, "do you think he

found one? That sounds like the wood on the bone-sticks, doesn't it?"

"He could have painted those to look that way," Sal said. "I've tried to tell you, Grandpa was—"

"Crazy!" Thea said. "You tell us all the time. But he was also brilliant. What if he left the pieces of a dowsing rod so we'd put them together? So we would find something important."

"Whoa!" Wendell cleared his throat and shoved his crooked glasses up higher on his nose. He pointed to a passage in the book. "So it says h-here that dowsing rods are also known as w-water witches!"

"That's a witch that could lead the way!"

"To what?" Sal asked. "The river is dried up. There's an ocean, but we'll never find the treasure if he threw it in the ocean."

"Widows do watch the water," Thea said as she rubbed Ichabod's soft ears. "I asked Ms. Dorrie what she watched, and that was her answer. But if you stand on our widow's watch, you wouldn't see anything except the front yard and street. And the fountain. Of course if you look to the right, you'd see the O'Pinion house."

"Well, if the rest of the sticks are hidden in there,

we're really sunk," Sal said, flopping down in one of the old chairs in the room. On a typical Thursday night back at the swamp, they might tell stories, then slide down the bannisters, then stay up late and make midnight pancakes.

But this day was not typical. Their mood today was more solemn. They all knew what Desdemona had in mind for them. Even though the town was coming around to the Problim family, Desdemona O'Pinion would have them split apart and scattered all across the globe.

"I do think V-Violet was right on about the r-rainbow," Wendell said. "And Thea's right about the Theodora statue shining the right way. But how do we test that? We don't even know the season Grandpa wrote these clues."

Toot farted. A #104.[26]

"The s-sun shines at different angles in different seasons," Wendell told him. "So maybe it was p-pointing to a clue in the library when Grandpa wrote that clue. But there's no way we can know."

"And that'd take too long to figure out," Sal said.

---

26 #104: The Questioner: A fart demanding further explanation of a topic. Contains notes of spoiled milk and honeysuckle.

Frida walked across the floor on her hands, saying:

"We do not have seasons in which to seek.
We don't have months.
We don't have weeks."

The sound of sneakers barreling across the hallway made them all turn in unison toward the large doorway. Sundae rushed in with a sad look on her face . . . and a small bundle in her arms.

Sundae shook her head. "My letters all came back. And the others I've tried to send, via the Andorran government . . . they were returned," Sundae said. And everyone was nervous, even Sundae, who never faltered, who wasn't afraid to look Desdemona O'Pinion in the eye. Thea waited for her sister to put a positive spin on this, but it didn't happen.

"I have a confession," Sundae said. "I am beginning to worry. I've tried letters. I've tried email, but Andorra decided to have a technology-free season, so that was a bust. I can't even get through with a phone. But nobody fret! I do have one other plan in place that I'm sure will work!"

"We're doomed," Thea said, sinking down into

the old couch. "As soon as I saw the three sevens back at the bungalow. I tried to tell you—"

"Stop." Sundae held up a shaky hand. "Don't say what you were going to say. Say something wonderful instead."

Thea shook her head. "I can't. Because I don't feel it."

"Then say it until you feel it," Sundae told her.

Thea closed her eyes. She imagined three sevens fluttering around in the garden of her imagination, bright butterflies with sunny-colored wings. "Something wonderful," she whispered.

Frida pulled an aluminum foil crown from her hair and placed it on Thea's head. She whispered:

"Wonderful,
lovely,
bright and true.
Marvelous things can happen too."

Ork-ork. Ichabod brushed against her leg.

"Something wonderful." Sundae hugged the letters to her heart. "Let's keep believing that, all right? Grandpa left something wonderful for us to find.

And Mom and Dad will come home." She grinned. "Problems solved."

Wendell nodded. "W-wonderful."

"Wonderful," Sal mumbled, staring at the dust-covered statue of Theodora Problim.

⁓

While her siblings continued to plot into the evening, Thea and Ichabod sat together in the Room of Constellations.

Twenty-one days was nearly up. Three sevens were at hand. There was no proof of their Problimness in the mansion, only three random bone-sticks that might lead somewhere. In the beginning, Thea had only half believed that something might separate them. Weeks ago, the Problim children were happy swamp rats. Now they were potential orphans.

Something wonderful . . . she kept reminding herself.

Something wonderful . . .

Maybe that's what it takes to find a treasure, she thought. Just the bold, nearly silly belief that you actually can. Maybe true treasure hunters in the world weren't just good at reading maps or piecing together a crazy grandpa's crazier clues.

Maybe it had to do with believing the impossible, with seeing the world heart-first.

And Thea Problim was part of a legacy of people who saw more than what was there. "It is what it is," she'd heard people say with resignation. But the Problim children had never believed that statement. For them, a problem was just a challenge. Things weren't always as they seemed. Any situation has the potential to be better.

Something wonderful . . .

"Please come home." Thea pointed a flashlight toward the ceiling and smiled at the sight. Someone—Grandfather?—had painted all those constellations of sparkling, silver stars. It had taken hours, probably. She pushed open the old window in the room, hoping to see the real stars that might have inspired him long ago. Although she was less afraid of heights now, her fear wasn't totally gone. She took a shaky step back.

Storm clouds rumbled, low and deep over the city. The lights from homes in the Cove sparkled. The church bell chimed, signaling another day's end. Those were good ways to mark time, Thea decided: stars and church bells and the colors of evening, rising above the shadow mountains. The call of a lark and the last wink of a setting sun. Those were good markers because they always came back; they continued. Good-bye was a terrible way to end a day. Because good-bye meant "The End."

Thea moved a little closer to the open window. She knew that lots of girls might stand in that same spot and imagine they were princesses, looking out over their starry kingdoms. But Thea imagined she was a brave knight, a dazzling sword fighter with a horse named Moonbeam. She'd tame dragons and ride their backs. She'd find her parents—and whatever they were doing—and help keep them safe. She would bring them home.

"Thea?" Wendell whispered from the secret passage doorway.

Her heart settled at the sound of him approaching.

"Don't the houses look pretty at n-night?" Wendell asked. He jumped up in the window seat and held out his hand.

She hesitated.

"Allergic to gravity," she reminded him. "It's always bringing me down!"

Wendell rolled his eyes. His hand remained

extended. Something about her brother would always make her feel a little bit braver than she knew she could be.

"I can't," she told him. "You might not be able to keep me from falling."

"T-trust me?" he asked.

Tentatively she climbed into the seat. A flimsy screen separated them from the night, the kind of screen with bug guts smooshed in the squares. But past the screen and the bug wings, their eyes adjusted to the darkness. And they could see for miles. She saw a dark patch she knew to be the Bagshaw Forest, where she'd explored last night. Where she'd met a new friend. That had been something wonderful, hadn't it? Maybe wonderful wasn't *so* far away . . .

A dark cloud peeled away from the sky, revealing the steady light of a wishing star. Wendell quoted, "Wishing star, I wish them home. . . ." He looked longingly at the night.

"Back to the place where they belong," Thea added. And then she sighed. "We sound like Frida."

"Didn't Grandpa tell us a story about a w-wishing star?" Wendell asked.

Thea squeezed her eyes shut and searched through her memories. "Yes! We were sitting together on the front porch of the bungalow. We were so tiny then, little enough to fall asleep on his shoulders. And he pointed to the brightest star. It was docked in the waves of one of those glory-glory sunsets. You know the kind I mean—where the clouds look like waves, rippled with pink and gold and darkest blue?"

Wendell nodded. "He told us that the wishing star was actually a b-boat."

"Right! And that boat held a captain. And he said that the captain sailed the sky—always. Just fishing for wishing."

Wendell smiled.

"Do you wish we could go back home?" Wendell asked. "Back to the Swampy Woods?"

"I loved it there," Thea said. "But no, that's not my wish. I want us all to stay together, always, exactly the way we are. I want us to have a thousand adventures. Together."

Wendell sighed. They listened to the crickets chirp for a while. And then Thea added, "And some-times . . ." She twisted her fingers together. "Maybe on our own. That's nice too."

Wendell nodded. His mouth quirked into the shadow of a grin. Wendell stuck out his fist. "Th-thump?" he asked softly.

"Bump," she said with a smile as she bumped her hand against his. "I wish Mom and Dad would just come home."

And she imagined the wish floating up and up, to the place where the captain of the wishing boat fished it from the skies.

"They will," he assured her.

"We're going to find the rest of the sticks," she said. "And figure out where they lead."

"I believe it. I believe in you too. Look at y-you! Up here in the w-window seat!"

"I feel brave when you're around." Thea shrugged.

"S-same here."

Thump, *bump*.

A Way In

Later that day, Violet O'Pinion was still thinking about her new friends. She hadn't had a chance to sneak and see them again—yet—but she kept them close to her heart. Violet sketched the Problim riddle into her favorite notebook, the one she usually reserved for drawing plants and butterflies and monuments around the world.

> *Mr. Biv will show the way,*
> *Where widows watch is where he stays.*
> *Nestled there inside the beast,*
> *Is the first clue for which you seek . . .*

She was listening to music too. Fun, wacky music that reminded her of the Problim children. She bopped her head and made more notes about the clues. She thought about treasure hunting and some kind of beast and other glorious things she'd never seen from her tower room. Biscuit hopped up in Violet's lap and licked her chin. Violet paused long enough to scratch Biscuit's fluffy ears and kiss her forehead.

So she did not hear the door open.

She didn't notice anyone was in the room until she saw her aunt Desdemona's shadow filling up her desk.

Violet slapped down her hand on the notebook, but it was too late. She only ripped off the corner of the page as Desdemona stole it away. Biscuit pounced up on the desk and growled, baring a row of tiny teeth.

"Interesting, this," Desdemona said.

"It's nothing," Violet told her. "I was writing a story—"

"Sweet girls like you don't lie, Violet." Desdemona scanned the page, and it was as if each line she read pulled the smile across her face wider. Wolfish, almost.

"You are being cruel," Violet whispered. She'd

never talked back to her aunt before. But then, she barely spoke to her aunt at all.

Desdemona looked up over the page. She cocked her head to the side. "Excuse me?"

"You're so mean to the Problims. They aren't hurting you. They only need a place to live, and their parents are—"

"And how do you know all this? Did you leave your room, as you were specifically instructed never to do?"

Violet clamped her mouth shut.

Desdemona smiled. "I believe you did. And I think they told you all about the little treasure hunt they're having in that grand old house. Tell you what, Miss Viii-olet." Desdemona ripped the page from the book. "I'll keep this. And in exchange, I won't tell your father you've been sneaking out to spend time with the dangerous neighbors."

"They're not dangerous!"

Desdemona tossed the notebook back on Violet's desk. "They are, Violet. And they were far too trusting. If they truly are Problims, they should know that Problims and O'Pinions have troubles. And those troubles go back farther than any of you could understand."

"Which means they're pointless," Violet said. "And it's time to get over it!"

"There is a treasure in that house, Violet. If not a treasure, there is a map there. Or a key or a legend or something that will lead to it. Frank Problim—that old rat—he took something from the town safe years ago. And that something was marvelous. A treasure that would make us wealthy beyond our wildest dreams. And not just wealthy . . . if it's what I think it is, it could change everything."

Violet had never seen such a dangerous gleam in her aunt's eyes.

Desdemona held up the ripped page. "Can't you feel it? Can't you see that you want it too?"

Violet shook her head. "I only wanted to help them find it. I only want a friend."

"Tsk." Desdemona walked back to the stairs, her shadow stretching long behind her. "That's unfortunate. Because once they know you gave me this, well . . . they won't want to be your friends."

A tear trembled in Violet's eyes.

"Go back to your books and maps and dreaming, Violet," Desdemona said, a menacing softness in her voice. "There's nothing outside this world you need to be part of. Nothing a girl like you will ever need to see."

As the door shut, Violet gulped deep breaths of purified air—all she'd ever get to breathe. Biscuit barked twice at the door, growled a last time, and then pounced back into Violet's lap. Violet held Biscuit close; her tears matted the dog's fur. But Biscuit didn't mind. Dogs never do. *That's what fur is for,* Biscuit would have said, if she had a voice. She didn't, of course. But until the Problims had come into her life, Biscuit was the only one who'd looked at Violet like she wasn't a freak. She'd looked at her like she loved her.

"I love you too," she sniffled.

Violet stood and looked at the maps on her walls. England. An African desert. Coastlines and causeways and mountains with jagged, toothlike edges.

She noticed her own shadow, so small there against the wall of maps. And she wondered if that was as close as she'd ever get to the places she longed to go.

⚬⚬⚬

Desdemona hadn't even considered Violet would be so helpful in cracking the search for the Problim treasure. Had she known, she would have sent the child sooner. Violet! Calm, quiet, obedient Violet had snuck out of the house. And infiltrated the enemy home.

And uncovered this marvelous riddle. Where had the children found it? Not that it mattered now. What mattered was that she had it.

Desdemona walked into her office and turned on the lamp, holding the paper underneath as if she'd find some sort of invisible markings on it. She'd never been good with riddles. And that old geezer had loved them so. She'd never known a man named Mr. Biv. And *where widows watch*? How many widows were in town? And what would they watch? *Where* would the widows watch whatever widows watch? Should she check the retirement home? This was entirely too complicated and time-consuming for her. She needed to get back inside that house.

Sometimes, Desdemona decided, when you want a thing . . . when you really want a thing . . . you must be ruthless to get it.

But how to get them out?

Even Mrs. Timberwhiff was warming to the Problim children. She'd started that petition—at Desdemona's insistence—but had put it away after

the frilly-silly birthday party that Sundae Problim decided to throw. Granted, the neighbors still
thought the Problems were odd. Total freaks. But
Desdemona could tell they were warming to them.
Even the donut sisters! Just the other day, Bertha had
jogged past the house eating one of those terrifying
organic skull-shaped cookies the kids baked.

No, the neighbors would be of no help.

Desdemona looked down at the paper again, and
she noticed Violet's drawings up and down the sides.
She'd drawn the Problim family—and Violet had
drawn them well. Sundae was small and smiley. The
rest looked like dark-haired vampires.

Except . . . the pig. That stupid, smelly pig.

(*Actually*, Desdemona thought, *the pig didn't
seem to stink* that *much. But in general, pigs were
terrible creatures.*)

She'd seen them all with the pig at various times.
She'd seen the baby fall asleep at the birthday party,
hugging the pig like it was a sweet, fluffy teddy bear.

Ichabod, they called it.

"To solve this problem," she assured herself, "I
must be ruthless."

And she hatched a plan to get the Problems
out of the house. Out of the house and into a

dangerous situation that the Society for the Protection of Unwanted Children would actually see. The Problim children seemed parentless. They were wild delinquents, trying to take care of each other without having real schooling.

The Society needed to see that. Once they did, they'd ship the Problims off to other families—far, far away from Lost Cove. And then, finally, the Problim family would be gone for good.

Mr. Biv Shows
the Way

"I don't know why you care if the house is clean," Sal said to Sundae as he grudgingly carried a basket of cleaning supplies down the spiral stairs. "We're going to lose it anyway to that troll next door if we don't leave. I think it's time we jump ship. Go hide in the swamp until Mom and Dad get back."

"Nice try," Sundae said. "You still have to clean it."

"Have you heard from Mom and Dad?" Sal asked.

"Not yet. But I will. I have a backup plan that's foolproof. Plan Feline, I call it."

"We're out of time, Sundae! We have a day left. One day! Whatever Plan Feline is, it needs to happen now."

"Preparation is everything," Sundae said, and she headed for another room while Sal grudgingly polished the statue collection in the library.

He attached a dust cloth to the long, grabbing stick he kept attached to his upper arm. But gah, the books. Those would take forever to dust. Wendell had already pulled each book from the shelf and hugged it, introduced himself, and then put it back as gently as if it were a sleeping dragon snapper. Sal decided that was the same as dusting.

So he returned his attention to cleaning the statues; Theodora Problim, in particular. He gave the lantern a quick swipe with his dust rag and then moved on to the next room. He didn't notice the way the sun hit the lantern just right, illuminating again a fine, rainbow line . . .

꧁

Toot waddled around on the marble floors of the foyer. His plans for the day were to teach Ichabod how to fetch, then take a nap, then eat, then play with the pig again.

Ichabod slowly waddled over with the yellow tennis ball Toot had tossed. Toot kissed the pig's snout, then patted its head.

Ichabod snorted suddenly and hopped backward.

Toot turned around so quickly that he flopped down on the floor . . . just in time to see Carley-Rue O'Pinion sneak past the window.

Using Ichabod for balance, Toot stood up again and popped a #6.[27]

Mona came running into the room, ponytail swishing behind her. "Hello, Toot. I've built a human cannon, and you're the perfect size for my test launch. Are you busy?"

Her nose wrinkled. "Oh no."

Toot reached for her with grabby hands, and she pulled him into her arms. He pointed to the window, and she ran for the front door, opening it to look around. Carley-Rue's crown sparkled in the sun.

"Ooh," Mona cooed happily. "It's the Hot Dog Queen."

~~~~~~~~~~~~~~~~~~~~

27 #6: The Paul Revere: A trumpetous fart of warning. One toot if by land. Two toots if by sea. Smells of cruciferous vegetables.

At the sight of Mona, Carley-Rue squealed. And ran.

"Stay here, Toot." Mona sat him down quickly and took off in a sprint after Carley-Rue.

Toot grinned and clapped. Carley-Rue would never outrun Mona. And definitely never outplot her. Whatever Carley-Rue was doing, her evil plan had been thwarted.

Then, from the foyer, Toot heard a voice say, "Come here, piggy, piggy . . ."

He turned around in time to see Ichabod lunge for a Cheeto that Desdemona was holding. Once the pig was close enough, she snatched him and ran. Toot waddled after her as fast as he could, chin trembling, popping a series of distress farts all the way to the spiral stairs.

Toot Problim was probably the bravest of all his brothers and sisters. Only time would tell, of course. But he never looked back, even when help didn't come. He followed Desdemona up the stairs, tottering and crawling up, up, toward the attic . . . the room Sal told him to stay away from at all costs. Toot would protect Ichabod.

Wendell and Thea sat crisscross on the floor of the library, poring over the purple book.

Sal plopped down beside them. "Find anything helpful?"

"Wendell might be onto something," Thea said.

"You've heard of the f-four elements?" Wendell explained. "Fire, water, earth, air?"

"Of course," Sal said.

"So, this book says ancient civilizations th-thought there were actually three more. Seven total. The sun, the moon, and metal. Gold, in p-particular. Like treasure!"

Sal shrugged. "Desdemona O'pinion doesn't look like someone who gives a hoot about ancient civilizations. Or modern ones, even."

Wendell pushed his crooked glasses higher on his nose. "Here's s-something interesting. Some civilizations believe that these elements are connected to the days of the week. That a person is naturally drawn to whatever element represents the day they were b-born on."

"That sounds pretty hokey," Sal said. He pulled duct tape from his belt and reached over to repair the book's spine.

"And y-yet." Wendell smiled, flipping gently through the pages of the book. "Saturday—your day—has to do with the earth. Someone connected to the earth can make it produce things, make it d-do things. Like you can. Until we moved here to Lost Cove, I thought fog m-monsters were common. But they aren't."

Sal leaned closer. "But there are lots of other people born on a Saturday. So why couldn't they do the same thing?"

"We thought about that!" Thea answered. "They probably can do it, at least a little bit. But do you remember how Mama always said we were a perfect seven? The scroll Grandpa left in the squirrel read *where seven seek, a treasure waits*. Not just one person—but all of us. And he told us to always remember our birthday rhyme! So maybe we are able to do . . . special things because we're together?"

"C-consider this," Wendell said. "Who can open any lock?"

Sal pointed to Thea as she raised her hand.

"Metal!" Wendell said, pointing to the book. "Metal is the element for someone born on a Th-Thursday."

"And Wendell's element," Sal murmured as he flipped through the pages. "Water?"

"Apparently." Wendell shrugged. And shivered. "Which is strange, because I dream about water all the time. Sometimes in a g-good way! And sometimes I dream that the house is f-flooding or that we're stuck in a r-raging river or something . . ."

"Fine," Sal said. "But why does Desdemona O'Pinion care?"

"She cares," Thea explained, "because together, we can do anything. Maybe even find a treasure. I think she knows exactly what Grandpa hid. And she knows we can find it."

"Wait!" Sal turned the page to a full-color illustration. "I've seen this before. Follow me!"

Sal found a tall ladder and carried it to the foyer. He climbed to the only window he'd never gotten around to removing the boards from—the circular, pie-piece window. He pulled his crowbar from his sleeve and began to pry the nails loose.

The first board fell off, and a bright beam of light reached through the glass.

"Purple," she said, blinking at the purple pie-shaped wedge of window Sal had uncovered. On the window was a symbol that caught her eye: an ocean wave.

"Whoa!" she and Wendell declared at the same time, staring down at the book. That same symbol was illustrated on the page.

"This window looks like a stained-glass pizza full of those same symbols," Sal said, jumping back to the ground and racing toward them.

The sun drifted across the floor, into the library, all the way to Theodora Problim's statue. But this time, it did not end there. It shone against her newly polished mirrored lantern and bounced off the far wall, creating a zigzag rainbow beam of light to the chandelier and out the window.

The rainbow path bounced off the purple-tailed squirrel, which sat in a tree outside.

Mr. Biv will show the way.

Few things were more frustrating to Sal than being so close to an answer—dancing all around it—and still not knowing what to do.

"Look!" Thea yelled as she noticed the rainbow pathway. She ran to the window and pushed it open to lean outside. She needed to see the Porch of Certain Death from underneath. Sal leaned over beside her, his tools pressing into his arms as he did.

"We've looked up there," Sal said. "Wendell and I climbed up and rappelled down this house."

"Where widows watch," Thea said. Not *what* the widows watch. *Where* they watch. *On* the Porch of Certain Death!"

"Problims, pile up!" Thea yelled, shoving away from the window.

Footsteps bounded down the stairs.

"The treasure is *on* the Porch of Certain Death!" Thea yelled as her siblings ran into the room.

Sal scratched his head. "It's a bunch of rotten boards and rails. The only things up there are Beethoven and Leroy—the gargoyles Wendell and I decorated for the birthday party."

Wendell thought for a moment. "The clue says that the treasure is inside the monster's beak! I didn't l-look at them very closely. Treasures are all different sizes, right? What if it's inside one of them?"

"So we need to climb up there and explode some statues?" Sal said.

Wendell shook his head excitedly. And then they all cheered. Climbing! Explosions! That sounded like a perfect Problim day!

And then . . . they all fell silent. Because they smelled a #1.[28] A distress fart.

The odor was coming from somewhere up above them. Far above them. From the general direction of the Porch of Certain Death.

---

28 #1: The I-Want-My-Mommy Fart: Smells like spoiled milk and mashed bananas. Toot's most desperate plea in times of deepest distress.

254

Toot's Watch

Sundae leaned out the window, stretching so far that Frida grabbed on to her ankles so she wouldn't fall out. Sundae swiveled around, looking up at the porch. The boards heaved and splintered slowly as a baby crawled over the top. "Oh no! Tooty-kins! TOOT! What are you doing up there?"

"Toot's up there?" Sal squeezed out beside her. "How did he get up into the attic?"

Sundae didn't answer. She was too busy running for the stairs to get to him. "He's on the Porch of Certain Death, Sal! He'll fall right through!"

Sal and Frida followed her.

"I'll go down below in case he falls, so I can catch

him!" Wendell yelled, thundering down the stairs. "S-stay there, Thea! So we'll have someone in the middle."

"Don't crawl, Toot!" Thea yelled from the window. "Just STOP!" But Toot was focused on something, crawling faster over the boards. She could hear the boards popping, even under her baby brother's slight weight. She realized he wasn't alone up there when she heard something *ork-ork*ing anxiously.

So Thea did not hesitate.

She stood on the window seat. She reached for the rope Wendell used to rappel from that old house. She felt gravity pulling her toward the ground. But her fear of falling from a high place was replaced by the greatest fear of all: seeing one of her siblings hurt. Fear wasn't holding her back now. It was giving her the push she needed to go.

Or maybe it wasn't fear pushing her. Maybe it was love. Maybe her love for Toot was big enough to squish out her fear of anything else.

Thea wrapped the rope around her waist and climbed out the window. She pressed her feet against the side of the house as she'd seen her brothers do, and climbed upward as fast as she could. Maybe she had finally conquered her fear of heights for good!

. . . And then she made the mistake of looking down. This looked exactly like the scene in her dreams. Falling, falling with no one beside her, and no one to hold on to her. Dizziness overwhelmed her. The edges of her vision became fuzzy.

Her feet slid.

She gripped the rope tightly as her body smacked against the wall.

The boards of the Porch of Certain Death wheezed above her as Toot moved across them.

"Stop crawling, Toot!" she yelled.

Her feet were making bicycle circles in the air. Maybe this moment was the terrible-awful thing she knew was bound to happen. Her baby brother—and Ichabod—were about to fall through the Porch of Certain Death. She was dangling from a rope. Her parents were missing. The Society for the Protection of Unwanted Children would be coming for them, and soon. She was alone. Gripping the rope, Thea tried to think of some quote from Midge Lodestar's show that would give her courage. But then:

Thump, *bump. I believe in you.*

Her eyes blinked open and looked down again.

Wendell was standing below, watching her, with his hand over his heart.

Thump, *bump*.

"I can't be fearless," she whispered.

You're better than fearless, Wendell thought. *You're brave. Keep climbing! You don't have far to go.*

Thursday's child has far to go. What if "far to go" didn't mean she was always trying to catch up with everyone else?

What if it meant she could go anywhere she wanted? What if it meant she was limitless?

"Thursday's child . . . ," she said, gripping the rope, "is brave and courageous." Her feet found the wall again. "Every day is a good day for a taco!"

That was the best part of having such a huge family: you were loved by all those crazy hearts. And you're never alone when you're loved. For them, she would be brave. She *was* brave. And she scampered up the side of the Problim mansion even faster than a robo-squirrel. "Toot! Hold on! I'm on my way!"

She set her eyes on the widow's watch, on her baby brother crawling there and the pig trembling on the edge. Her arms burned as she pulled on the rope.

"Thea?" Sundae yelled for her. She was still tip-toeing across the support beams in the attic. "Is that you?"

"Don't walk out here!" Thea said. "It'll crumble under your weight! I've almost got him."

Suddenly Sal and Frida appeared on the roof, standing on the gable. Sal was lassoing a long rope of Wrangling Ivy, his eyes on Toot, who was just out of reach.

"I've got Toot!" Thea called.

Frida shouted:

"Yes, yes!
We see!
The baby's fine!
Fear not, dear sister!
We'll get the swine!"

Wendell's voice rose from the ground again. He shouted, "Thea Problim! I b-believe in you!"

"I believe in me too," she whispered.

One hand in front of the other, Thea finally climbed up beside the Porch of Certain Death. Toot reached out his arms, and she snatched him close, hugging him tightly. Sal and his Wrangling Ivy retrieved the trembling Ichabod . . . just as the board the pig had been trembling on cracked loose from the house and crashed to the ground.

"Move, Wendell!" Thea yelled.

Fortunately, her twin had enough sense on his own to do just that.

Thea sighed. Toot was a stinky bundle of snuggles whose arms were almost choking Thea. She nearly cried in relief.

Sal yelled from above her, "You can just rappel down the house now, if you feel okay doing that. Rope's secure. Wendell installed it."

Thea nodded. She was about to go, when she noticed the googly-eyed gargoyle, Leroy. The one Sal and Wendell had decorated for the party. One of the eyes slid sideways to reveal a strange shine. Thea's heart fizzed with hope.

"Love you, stink pot," she said, kissing the baby on the head and passing Toot through the window to Sundae.

Sundae smiled. "Well, how's that for a fun afternoon, Tooty-kins?"

Thea used her body's momentum to swing back toward the porch, where she scaled the wall sideways

toward Leroy. The gargoyle still had on the googly-eyed glasses from the party. She grabbed its neck with one arm and pulled them off. But there was nothing beneath; the sparkle she'd seen was just in the stone itself.

Look again, she could hear her mother whispering. *Look heart-first.*

There was more there than what she was seeing. She could feel it. There inside the monster's beak . . .

There was nothing in that gargoyle's mouth, so she shimmied to the other side.

"What are you doing?" Sal called.

There! She saw something sparkle, shiny as a wishing penny. She wiped the caked dirt and mud away from the gargoyle's mouth and dislodged a small silver tube. And there was something else behind it, something long and twiggy and wrapped in velvet.

Toot squealed from the window. Ichabod *orked* safely beside him.

"We got it together," she said to Toot. "You found the treasure, Toot! Or . . . whatever this is."

He smiled proudly and popped a celebratory

#115.²⁹ And he reached for her.

"You want to ride down with me?"

Toot applauded.

She reached for him and held on tight. Together, they rappelled down to the grassy world below.

This time Thea didn't look up or down, she looked all around her.

Toot giggled as Thea pointed out the mountains in the distance. They saw fog rising from the Bagshaw Forest. She'd been in there, she realized. And she couldn't wait to explore more of it.

Thursday's child could do that. Thursday's child could go anywhere.

Adventure had snagged her heart, and now she'd never settle for less. She would always be afraid of something. But she would always be courageous too. A warm wind blew gently over her forehead, and she laughed, imagining it was a fuzzy-mustache kiss from Grandpa Problim. *Make your life the best story you'll ever tell.* He would be so proud of her.

---

29 **#115**: The Confetti Fart: Makes a high-pitched trumpet sound. Released to mark a moment of celebration. Smells like rotten potatoes.

My *bold adventurers*—that's what he always called Problim children. *My daring dreamers.*

Thea and Toot touched down to the ground, into the waiting arms of their siblings.

And just as they locked tight in a hug, Toot tooted a terrified #6.[30]

Desdemona O'Pinion, the mayor, and seven men and women in wrinkly black suits came marching around the house.

Sal's voice trembled. "See those badges they're wearing?" he whispered. "That's the Society for the Protection of Unwanted Children."

The mayor was arguing at every step. "Give the parents another day or two! Who came up with this twenty-one-day rule anyway? The children aren't hurting anyone."

"They're a danger to the neighborhood and quite obviously to themselves. Look up there!" Desdemona pointed to where the widow's watch used to be . . . but she seemed surprised to see it crumbled to the grass. She was even more shocked to see the Problim family all together, safe on the ground.

---

30 #6: The Paul Revere: A trumpetous fart of warning. One toot if by land. Two toots if by sea. Smells of cruciferous vegetables.

"You're behind this," Sal said, standing in front of his family. "You put Ichabod on the walk so Toot would crawl out after him!"

Desdemona ignored him. "As you can see from the state of things, this is no home for children. Especially these children. They're drifters. They're poor. They have no money, no propriety, no manners . . ."

"Excuse you," Sundae said exasperatedly.

Toot puffed a #47.[31]

"See," Desdemona said proudly. Her voice rose steadily. "They're liars, orphans. They have no parents. Look at the knives on that boy's arms!"

"They're gardening tools!" Sal shouted. He pulled off his faithful pruning shears and demonstrated.

Desdemona snarled. "They've been parading as a rich old man's kinfolk so they can have his house, but it's not theirs to have anymore. It's day twenty-one, and they're as orphaned as they were on the day they came. They are unwanted."

It was the greatest lie she told; they all knew it. To be wanted by one person in the world was enough to make life good, but to be wanted by your

---

31 **#47**: The Defensive-Offensive: A toot used by Toot that creates an invisible, yet rancid, cloud of protection around those he loves.

parents and six other siblings was a treasure beyond compare.

"Our parents are archeologists," Sundae said calmly to the officer. "They've been knighted by the Queen of Andorra herself, and they search for strange and unusual artifacts. In cases of extreme need, I'm allowed to—"

"Young lady," the man looked truly apologetic. "I'm afraid I can't let you stay here with no parents. It just isn't right. We'll have to take you to Children's Services."

Take them. All of them. In different cars, to different places.

Thea Problim felt the wildness stirring up inside her. "No," she shouted, stepping in front of her siblings and stretching out her arms. Her siblings all reached back. The scene reminded her of the day the bungalow had shattered; except now it wasn't a house falling apart. It was her family falling apart. And this time, she wouldn't cower on the ground. She would look her problems in the eye. And she couldn't—she wouldn't—let her own Problims go.

"I don't have a choice," said the officer.

Desdemona smiled triumphantly.

An old Volkswagen van pulled up to the house.

The side door opened, and thirteen cats wearing tiny backpacks meowed as they jumped.

Carley-Rue opened her arms and squealed. "Miss Florida 1987? That's my cat!" The calico cat jumped into her arms and licked her face. The other cats dispersed, heading back to their neighborhood homes.

Sundae looked after them hopefully. "I knew the felines would find them!"

Desdemona shouted at her, "I knew you were stealing the cats!"

"I didn't steal them," Sundae said. "Cats are born adventurers. They have excellent memories and can travel for thousands of miles. Any cat can be a carrier cat if it believes in its calling."

"Sundae," Sal said. "Who are you talking about? Who did you send the cats to find?"

Sundae's eyes filled with tears. A quivering smile stretched over her face. "Mom and Dad."

The door of the van slammed. And a familiar voice that settled their souls yelled, "Kids? What happened?"

Major

"**D**ad!" Thea and Wendell yelled, running into his arms.

Desdemona's mouth fell open. She took off her sunglasses, revealing pale-brown eyes that looked much more sensitive than the rest of her. "Impossible . . . ," she whispered. And then, more quietly, "Terrible man."

But he was not terrible at all, actually.

He was wonderful.

Major Problim, archeologist of fine relics for the Queen of Andorra and proud father to the seven Problim children, was really there. He was covered in dust and long-bearded from all his recent traveling. His dark eyes were lined with worry, but he was there. And his arms were as warm and strong as they'd ever been, long enough to hold all seven of them in a tight hug as they crowded around him. Toot puffed a #124[32] when Major lifted him into his arms.

"I missed you too, buddy," he said against Toot's forehead. Then, with his children around him, Major Problim turned, glaring at the officers. "What's the problem here?"

"There are six Problims!" Desdemona seethed.

"Seven!" Frida shouted.

"Eight," said Major, and he pulled the fox in for a hug. "Nine, when Mom gets here."

Mayor Wordhouse smiled. "We are delighted to see you, sir. It's been way too long. Let's chat about this over here, shall we?"

Major passed Toot to Sundae, and followed the mayor. But he stopped in front of Desdemona. "Dezi," he said softly. "Were you trying to send them away?"

She looked at him as though she were seeing a ghost.

---

32 **#124:** The Joyful, Joyful: Simple flatulence of happiness. Smells like a week-old bouquet of daisies.

She put her sunglasses back on and became the spider woman again.

"How was I supposed to know they were really yours? You let them run around like wild animals with no parents. I guess you deserted them like you did everyone else."

"I would never desert my children." Major said. "You know this is our home. The kids just came a little early." With sadness in his eyes, Major Problim added, "You aren't welcome here, Desdemona. You should leave. Now."

"Don't get comfortable here," Desdemona said. "This is not over. Some people forget things, Major. But I do not forget. And I definitely don't forgive."

"You used to."

She stopped at his words, her shoulders stiff and pulled back. "Some of us know when to grow up," she told him. Then she stomped back to her house next door.

As Major chatted with the mayor and the representatives from the society, the Problim children huddled close together.

Sundae said, "I don't think we should tell him about the treasure. Or the book. Not yet."

Sal nodded. "Grandpa wanted us to find it. He

gave us the secret, not our parents."

That would have made more sense, though, Thea thought. If Grandpa had entrusted this secret to their parents. They uncovered relics for a living. But he hadn't. *Where seven seek, a treasure waits.* That's what he said.

"Maybe he wasn't mad," Sal said, his voice soft and hopeful. "Maybe he was . . . brilliant."

"Dad," Thea said as the mayor and the society members walked away. "Where's Mom? Why did you come alone?"

"She's close behind me," Major said, a little too quickly. And then he barely whispered the words that sent shivers up her spine. "I hope."

Thea Problim gulped. She whispered to Wendell, "Everything's not okay. Not for good."

"But at least for n-now," he said softly.

De Léon

Once Major Problim had gone to bed, the children climbed up to the Room of Constellations.

"Put everything we've found in the middle," Sundae said.

Sal added his key necklace. Wendell added the purple book about the elements. Thea added all the new sticks they'd retrieved. Leroy's twig looked the same as the other ones they possessed: long and white, heavy when held, and gold at the edges. "That's four total now," she said.

Sal nodded as he picked up the sticks to study them. "The squirrel's clue said there were seven total. Put them together and they form, well, an even longer stick. Like the one in the painting."

"Like a w-water witch," Wendell added.

"And," Thea said. "We have this tube." She popped it open. "It looks like a . . . flash drive?"

The squirrel bounced into the room then, and winked at her.

Thea inserted the drive into the squirrel's eye. The creature went perfectly still and projected a film onto the dark wall. A countdown began:

7 . . . 6 . . . 5 . . . 4 . . . 3 . . . 2 . . . 1 . . .

And then, a voice the Problim children hadn't heard in years projected from the squirrel's speaker-ears:

"Hello, my daring daydreamers! My bold adventurers! I've got a tale worth telling you . . ."

Thea gasped. Sundae put her hands over her mouth. Frida clapped happily and Sal, Wendell, and Mona just stared as their grandpa's kind, wrinkly face filled the screen.

"He's th-there!" Wendell said, pointing to the wall. The children moved closer to the projection, looking up at his kind, old face. And he'd paused on the film, as if he was waiting just for that. His message had been filmed long ago, but the look in his eyes was the same loving look they remembered.

Maybe he was imagining their reaction. Certainly, he was thinking of his grandchildren.

"If you are watching this," Grandpa began, "I know these things are true. First, I know you are all together—and that there are seven of you now. Second, I know my squirrel did its job. Well done, Snookums!"

The squirrel flicked its tail proudly.

"Third . . . I know that dark days are ahead. But I'm here to tell you children—there is also a wondrous adventure ahead. The fact that you're watching this means I am not there with you—not physically—to help you through it. I'd always hoped to tell you this story in person. And maybe I can someday! Maybe I can tell you part of it, at least. As you might have noticed by now, our family is . . . different."

Frida asked:

"Let's pop some popcorn?
Make some munchies!
This movie's great, and the fox is hungry!"

"Not yet," Sundae smiled, pulling her close. "You don't want to miss anything, do you?"

Grandpa cleared his throat and continued,

"There's a story I haven't told you yet. And it's high time you hear it. 'Where seven seek, a treasure waits.' Our family has been proving this true for centuries. Every so often, a generation has a group of seven. The seven siblings belonging to Horatio Problim were pirates—good pirates, I might add. They found some of the greatest wonders of the world. The seven siblings belonging to Imogene Problim went in search of the tombs of the pharaohs. And my brothers and sisters . . . there were seven of us. And we found something too."

Sadness filled the old man's eyes. "We found a treasure in this very cove . . . and we made a decision to hide it. What I should have done . . . was destroy it. And you need to destroy it fast. There's someone else who wants it, see. And he's a clever old goat. Years ago, he found another group of seven and paid them handsomely to try to steal it from me. I took it before they could, of course. But there's a chance he's looking for pieces of the witch, just as eagerly as you are."

"Why can't he just tell us where it is?" Sal asked. "And why would he want us to destroy a treasure?"

"He's being cagey," Thea said. "Because he doesn't want someone else to find it."

Grandpa paused as if he'd heard the questions; he seemed to be choosing his next words carefully. "Any treasure worth finding is worth seeking. And you seek with your head and your heart—not just your dusty sneakers. And this treasure—" He shook his head. "Trust me, you won't understand what it means—and why you have to get rid of it—until you puzzle out this process. So be brave. Be daring. You are my bold adventurers and my daring dreamers. This is the first of many adventures you'll have together. See you soon." He winked.

And the film went dark.

For a time, the children sat in silence.

"We have to find the rest of the sticks," Wendell said. "And we have to be careful with the ones we have. They're s-so important." Wendell picked up a stick in each hand, and a surge of electricity shot up his arms.

"Wendell!" Thea cried, pressing her hands over her heart. "What's happening?'

The sound of water filled Wendell's ears, and strange scenes flashed through his imagination. A waterfall. A deep cave. A blue pool of water. And something, something hidden there . . . just behind the waterfall . . .

"Wendell!" Thea grabbed his arm.

And Wendell dropped the sticks. He blinked. He pulled off his glasses and pressed his hands hard against his eyes.

"What was that? What happened?" Thea asked. "Are you okay?"

Thump, *bump*.

"Yes." Wendell leaned down to look more closely at the sticks, pushing his glasses up on his nose.

"Guys," Wendell whispered, eyes dancing with excitement. His siblings leaned in closer. "De Léon will lead the way. What if he's t-talking about the fountain outside? The guy in the f-fountain!"

"Ponce de Léon?" Sal asked.

"Yes!" Wendell shouted. "P-Ponce de Léon! Do you remember what Ponce de Léon discovered?"

"The state of Florida?" Sal shrugged.

"Obviously that. But do you know what h-he was famous for? He was rumored to have discovered one other thing. A b-big thing. The Fountain of Youth."

Sal leaned in. "There's no way someone wouldn't have discovered something that big and kept it secret . . . especially around here."

"I'll bet a perfect seven could find it," Thea said softly. "What if that's where the water witch takes us? That's got to be what Grandpa wants us to find, right?"

A sneaky grin filled the face of Frida the Fox. "Ears up, buttercups," she whispered. "Adventure's afoot."

Wings Made of
Better Worlds

The next morning, Violet O'Pinion woke to find
Thea and Wendell Problim waiting outside her
window. She snapped on her helmet and opened the
window so they could crawl inside.

"I'm so sorry," she said immediately. "My aunt
made me give her the riddle!"

Thea shrugged. "We come up against problems
all the time. That's not why we're here."

Behind them on the zip line came a large cart full
of flowering plants.

"Don't worry." Thea smiled. "Sal engineered
these, and he's a pro. They have no smell and give off

only the best quality oxygen. So no need to worry about allergies. He said there are specific instructions for the dragon snappers . . ."

Violet nodded anxiously. "I know how to take care of them."

Wendell pulled out a book. "I know you p-prefer science to novels, but you'll like the girl in this book. She reminds me of you. She lives a grand adventure, and it all starts in her room."

"Thank you," Violet said softly. "You're good friends. Both of you."

Friends. Thea and Wendell smiled at the word. They had been each other's siblings forever, which was as good as a friend. But having friends beyond each other, that felt right too. Thea had a feeling they'd be having many more adventures with the astronaut next door.

Thump.

Bump.

⟲

Violet O'Pinion stayed awake late into the night. She tended to her black roses and dragon snappers and her tiny sprig of Wrangling Ivy, which she planned to use as the occasional escape route to visit the Problems.

And then she had an idea.

She pulled a box of art supplies from the closet.

She ripped the maps from her wall and worked through the night, cutting and pasting and molding . . . until her masterpiece was complete.

As the sun rose over Lost Cove, the light spilled warm and orange through Violet O'Pinion's window—illuminating the empty spot where the maps used to be.

"What do you think, Biscuit?" Violet asked.

The dog flapped her fuzzy ears in happiness.

Violet O'Pinion had fashioned those maps into a pair of paper wings. She fitted them over her shoulders and looked at herself in the mirror. She snapped on her helmet too.

The helmet had always reminded her of everything she absolutely could not do. But the wings reminded her of the Problim children. And the wings reminded her of the adventures she'd had in the past few days.

Maybe the air was dangerous. Maybe life was dangerous.

But even danger can't stop a true dreamer from dreaming.

There were many things in her lifetime that

Violet might not be able to do.

Oh, but there were far more things she could do. And perhaps it was time she focused on those things.

She turned to look at her shadow, silhouetted on the wall where the morning sun shone through. She liked this new shadow. She was still small, a fragile girl with a bubblehead . . . but the wings were what she noticed now.

She was no longer a girl made of glass.

She was a girl with wings made of worlds she'd never seen, places she'd never been. She was a girl ready for adventure. "Once upon a time starts here," Violet whispered. She was tired of waiting in her tower.

⚜

Violet wasn't the only happy O'Pinion in House Number Five.

Down in the basement, an old man sat in a wingback chair, one leg crossed over the other. His daughter paced back and forth behind the chair, mumbling about the Problim mansion and Major Problim and how she *loathed-hated-despised!* that wretched family. Especially Major.

"And that book you wanted," said Desdemona. "I was so close. I had it in my hand! The witch was right there on the front!"

The old man raised his hand. "Hush, dear. You'll find another way in."

"Yes," Desdemona said determinedly, her fists clenched at her sides. "I will."

Once he was sure she was gone, the man stood up slowly to his full height. He locked the door and went to the old desk in the corner of his office. Inside the top drawer, he pulled out an old purple book. Tucked inside the pages was something that looked like a piece of bone. Or maybe an old piece of tree bark. The tips were gold and the stick was heavy. He twirled it in his long fingers; it was cold and sturdy, and soon the rest of it would be in his possession. Surely the Problim children were already finding the other pieces. And once they'd found them all, he'd simply take what was his.

"You'll still lose, old friend," he said with a grin. He tucked the stick back into the book and hid it in the drawer. Then he smiled as he retrieved his violin from the corner. He played a song of madness, a song of memory, a song about days gone by and grudges that never grow old. And why should they?

The seven really had returned. The Problim children were back in House Number Seven.

Anything was possible now.

Acknowledgments

There are many friends who've walked beside me—all the way from the swamp to the cove— helping the Problim children tell their story. I am especially grateful to my editor, Maria Barbo, who encourages me, challenges me, and reminds me to have fun. I would also like to extend thank-you toots to Rebecca Aronson, Amy Ryan, Andrea Vandergrift, Emily Rader, Meaghan Finnerty, Ann Dye, Rosanne Romanello, Patty Rosati, Jill Amack, and, of course, to the swamptastic Katherine Tegen for her brilliant mind and creative heart.

My agent, Suzie Townsend, is the very best. I adore her, and would gladly launch her into the swamp on a human catapult anytime. The entire team of storybirds at New Leaf Literary has been so kind to me, especially: Joanna Volpe, Kathleen Ortiz, Mia Roman, Danielle Barthel, Sara Stricker, Pouya Shahbazian, and Chris McEwen. I'm also grateful for Bradley Garrett's work on behalf of my stories. Thank you all for taking such great care of my characters.

Teachers, librarians, booksellers, and bloggers who've helped my books find new homes also deserve heaps of thank-you farts. You're the ones making the real magic happen, and I'm honored you'd let any of my stories be part of your world.

Writing about seven kids who grew up in a magical swamp took me back home again. It reminded me of lazy days chasing butterflies and of the sound of willow tree branches clicking in the wind and of reading books on the back porch. And so, of course, I thought of the cousins and siblings I got to share those days with: especially Chase,[33] Melanie, and Michelle. They made every problem a wondrous adventure. Thanks for reminding me to stay wild inside my heart. I'm also forever indebted to my parents, Jim and Elaine, and to Bridgett, Ed, Erin, and Andy for giving me so much love and story-fodder, and for the new families I've added to my life this

---

[33] Various toots throughout this book may or may not have been inspired by this individual. If you have a brother, you understand.

year: the Longs, the Owensbys, the Manleys, the Seiferts, and the Dukes.

And I'm grateful to and for Justin, who is my best friend but better. You're more awesome than any story I could have imagined, and I love you.

I'm thankful to God for the wild, wonderful love of family and for new days full of new stories.

And I want to thank *you*, my fellow swamp flowers. Young readers often ask me about my favorite part of being an author. Making up stories is one part. Meeting young readers is a big part too. It's the heart part. Thank you for being brave enough to see the world heart-first, and for inspiring me to do the same. I hope you never forget how awesome you are. (And never forget: every day is a good day for a taco!)

Ears up, buttercups!
Adventure's afoot.
Don't miss the second
TOOT-TACULAR tale of

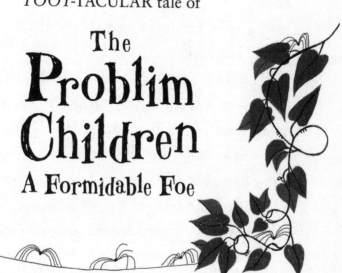

The Problim Children
A Formidable Foe

Everyone should have known better, really. The sky had gurgled storm warnings all morning long. But people still thought they had plenty of time to run to the store, the park, or the donut shop. Out for coffee, hot yoga, and cold yoga all before another storm settled over town.

They were wrong.

And most everyone was utterly miserable about

the wild weather except for two girls presently riding their bicycles down the sidewalk.

"Another puddle! GLORY!" Sundae Problim veered for a deep, muddy mess on the street, sliced through the middle and squealed as muck slopped up all over her jeans and shoes. She howled with happy laughter.

Her younger sister Mona Problim kicked along nearby on a scooter. She rolled her eyes at Sundae's latest nature exclamation: GLORY. That was Sundae's new thing; she shouted the word all the time these days. Mona quietly enjoyed the satisfying swish of her tires through the mud puddle, and the way the mud felt when it speckled her arms. So refreshing.

"Rain is my favorite weather," Mona called out. "Nothing like a nice, long walk in a thunderstorm."

The girls zoomed their bike (plus scooter) to a stop in front of the Good Donuts shop. The neon-pink "Open" sign seemed to flicker extra brightly against the darkening sky. Sundae skipped toward the entry. But Dorothy, the owner, met them at the door with her hands on her hips.

"STOP," Dorothy commanded. "Wipe your paws before you come into my shop." She pointed to the mat, then to a sign affixed to the building beside the door. "See here? No mud. No mess. No cell phones."

Sundae blinked. "I understand not wanting cell phones. But . . . mud is nature's love letter to all of us. Why not bring some of the joy of nature indoors?"

As Sundae began telling Dorothy about all the creatures who loved mud, Mona shimmied past her sister and into the bakery. The room smelled like warm cinnamon. Coffee sputtered from a machine in the corner. In the back of the room, fresh donuts zoomed off one conveyer belt, plopping down onto another. Then each one passed underneath a water-fall of white icing. *Rrrrr* . . . Now it was Mona's stomach rumbling, just as loud as the morning storm-sky.

Mona slid into a corner table beside her siblings. She wished she'd brought some circus spiders with her, to sneak one donut off the line. Not that her brother would let that happen. Wendell Problim stood guard over the donuts, wearing his new green apron and hairnet. He watched every circle of deli-ciousness roll past, counting each one, making sure they were iced appropriately. He'd been an intern at Good Donuts for a week now, and Sal had already helped him design a new, speedy conveyer belt.

The Turbo-Dough. Wendell's first job was counting inventory but he hoped to work his way up to Apprentice Decorator.

Mona couldn't wait until Wendell had access to the fryer, because that meant she'd have access too. She'd already thought about how many things she would like to deep fry. A boot. A book. One of Sal's plants. Maybe a spider.

Something bit Mona's thumb. Hard. A tiny, blue-legged circus spider glared up at her.

"I was kidding," she whispered. And then she grinned. "In fact, I'm so glad you're here. See that donut over there . . . ?"

"We'll figure it out," Sal said. "And then once it's together, we'll see where it leads us. If it leads us. Wendell says a water witch—this kind of twig—will pull you along to the place you need to go." Then he lowered his voice. "And I still think it will go somewhere magical."

"That's quite a hypothesis," Mona said, sitting taller to check the progress of the donut heist. One donut did appear to be magically crawling off the conveyer belt.

"How do we keep the spider lady from finding it first?" Thea asked. "And remember what Matilda said about Old Mr. O'Pinion? I think we need to find him. He sounds like the worst villain of all. If he finds it first . . ."

WHAP!!!

Bertha, owner of the donut shop next door, slammed a newspaper down on the table. "Kiddos! Have you seen this?"

Lost Cove Corn Dog Festival!
Who will brave the pirates' caverns?
Who will bake the year's prized pie?
Who will be crowned Little Miss Corn Dog?

"A p-pie competition!" Wendell said, startling them all.

Bertha nodded. "I do hope the rain stops before the festival kicks off."

The children all turned toward the sound of a happy "arf!" Biscuit, Violet O'Pinion's faithful dog, bounded into the room and shook the rain from her hair.

"No mud!" Dorothy said to the little pooch. But Biscuit ignored her. She pounced into Thea's arms. Sal reached for a tiny scroll attached to the collar around Biscuit's neck.

Come quickly!
I found something!
Bring me a donut.
      —Violet

"Problims, pile up!" Sundae shouted. And then she sweetly added, "Where is Tootykins?"